CHIPS

A HOMETOWN HERO

★

Based on the True-Life Adventures
of the World War II K-9 Hero

★

Nancy M. West

Off Lead Publications
980 Broadway, Suite 238
Thornwood, New York 10594

Reprinted 2007

ISBN 10: 0-9786722-5-9
ISBN 13: 978-0-9786722-5-6

Cover Illustration copyright © R. T. Foster 2004

Book Design by Jonathan Gullery

Previously published in the US by Hero Dog Publications (2004).
ISBN: 0-9743659-1-2

Library of Congress Cataloging in Publications Data: 2005935978

West, Nancy
Chips The War Dog: Based on the True Life Adventures of the World
War II K9 Hero/ by Nancy West
184p

    1.Young Adult. 2. Dogs. 3. Historical Fiction. 4. World War II.
    5. War Dog. 6. Home Front. 7. Dogs for Defense. 8. Chips. 9. Title

Printed in the United States of America

10 9 8 7 6 5 4 3 2

DEDICATED TO THE WAR DOGS

AND

THE MEN AND WOMEN WHO SERVE

A special thanks to Martha and Esther Linke
for their advice and encouragement.
Thank you also to Elizabeth Zack
and Judy Freed
for their gracious assistance.
And my sincere appreciation to Mr. John Wren
(who was once-upon-a-time
the little boy in the sailor's suit!)
for sharing his memories of Chips.

CONTENTS

★ ★ ★

"He didn't work with the idea of getting a cross or medal or a ribbon or extra pay—or even his name in the paper to make the crowds cheer at home.... He was just a soldier doing his job because that is what was asked of him. He could do this because he was a dog. A dog doesn't know enough to be anything but a *hero*."

<u>Bruce</u>, Albert Payson Terhune

MESSAGE TO
YOUNG READERS

This is a fictional account based on the real-life adventures of a dog that lived many years ago during the time when your grandparents or great-grandparents were kids just like you. It was a time when the world desperately needed heroes to fight for freedom and justice. Chips was one of those heroes.

★ ★ ★

Chips lay motionless on the frozen ground. His breaths were shallow and quiet. He had tried to follow the young dog, Torpedo, but each time he struggled to stand his left leg collapsed under him. Now he rested and waited until he had enough strength to find his way back to the camp. These were Rowell's final instructions to him: to find camp, to go home.

Home....

Chips's thoughts began to drift far away to another place and time. A time before he had gone to live with Rowell and the other soldiers. A place of innocence and peace...

★ ★ ★

CHAPTER 1

THE BEGINNING

It was Chips's first memory. He was curled up nose to tail with his six littermates in the cozy wooden crate next to the stove when Mrs. Larson, his human caretaker, burst into the kitchen with a bundle of bright red ribbons streaming from her arms.

"Time to get up, sleepy puppies," she said in her hearty voice. "Our party guests will be arriving soon, and you must all make a good impression." Mrs. Larson, an elderly but energetic woman, took in litters of puppies that had no families to care for them.

Chips yawned and stretched, first fore and then aft, as puppies do. He then pricked up his ears to follow the sound of Mrs. Larson's voice.

Chips liked Mrs. Larson. He liked the way she sang and whistled as she bustled around the warm, cheerful kitchen. He liked it when she reached into the old crate, picked him up in her arms, and gave him a scratch behind his ears or a tickle under his soft belly. But what

Chips particularly loved about Mrs. Larson were the leftover morsels of roast beef and other delicacies she fed to him while she cradled him in her arms.

On this morning Mrs. Larson was especially busy and excited. For nearly a week she had been preparing the house for her annual holiday party. She whistled a cheerful tune as she lifted one of Chips's sisters out of the crate, carried her to the kitchen sink, and dunked her in a tub of soapy bubbles. After scrubbing her thoroughly Mrs. Larson wrapped the puppy in a fluffy white towel and dried her off. Then she tied a bright red ribbon around her neck and put her back in the crate.

Chips eyed the colorful red ribbon and, thinking it was a toy, immediately lunged at the bow, ripping and tearing it off his squealing sister's neck.

"No, no, puppy!" Mrs. Larson gently scolded as she scooped Chips out of the crate and placed him on the kitchen table. "Why, you are the most mischievous imp I've ever seen. Someday your actions are going to get you into a heap of trouble. Don't you know that today is a special day? Families from the village are coming to our house. If you're lucky, one of them will take you away to live with them. Wouldn't you like to have a real home?"

Chips cocked his head to one side, trying to understand his caretaker's words. He had heard the word *home* mentioned from time to time in passing, but no one had ever emphasized it as strongly as Mrs. Larson did now. Chips concluded that *home* must taste very good to sound this important, and he wagged his tail in anticipation.

"Now, be a good puppy and you might find your own special family today," Mrs. Larson said as she lowered him into the sudsy tub of warm water.

The soap immediately stung Chips's eyes, and he coughed and sneezed as bubbles went up his nose. He shook his head vigorously to get the tickling sensation out of his ears, but his shaking was so forceful that Mrs. Larson lost her grip on the slippery pup and he flopped head first into the soapy tub.

Water filled Chips's mouth and nose, and he panicked. Sputtering and choking, he could no longer breathe. Before Mrs. Larson could grab hold of him, Chips pushed out his hind legs with all of his strength and leapt onto the kitchen floor, sending water and slippery soapsuds flying in all directions.

Mrs. Larson, who was a large, portly woman, let out a shriek! As she reached for Chips, her own feet flew out from underneath her on the now-wet floor, and she landed on her backside only inches from the frightened puppy.

Chips, having regained his breath, was so terrified of the screaming woman lying next to him that he immediately dashed for the kitchen door. He had nearly escaped when he ran head first into Mr. Larson's thick rubber boots.

"Well, well, what's all this about?" Mr. Larson exclaimed with surprise. He grabbed hold of Chips and raised him up with his strong hands. "Where do you think you're running off to, young fellow? And what are you doing sitting in a puddle of water on the floor, Mrs. Larson?" Having seen that his wife was unhurt, he knew the situation needed the help of a little humor.

"I must be a pretty sight," Mrs. Larson laughed good-naturedly as she pulled herself to her feet. But then her tone grew more serious. "In all honesty, I don't see how this pup will get along in a civilized household."

Chips rarely heard Mrs. Larson sound so concerned and he whimpered softly. Then Mr. Larson helped his wife hold Chips on the table while she dried him and tied one of the shiny red bows around his neck.

When she was finished she stood back to admire him. "Yet he is darling, isn't he? Look at the way his almond-shaped eyes tilt up. He always has a merry, impish look about him."

Chips's unruly ears drooped over to one side as he tipped his head and listened to Mrs. Larson's words.

Mr. Larson looked closely at the robust pup. "He has ears like a donkey's and that big black nose of his and the tan mask of fur around his eyes make him look like a clown. A clown in a black and tan fur suit," he chuckled.

Mrs. Larson sighed. "Perhaps he'll get into less mischief if he's not with the other puppies," she suggested, and she carried Chips down to the basement where she stored the extra dog crates.

Chips detested the dismal room below the kitchen. He had been crated there once before when the veterinarian, Dr. Brown, had come to examine all the puppies. On that occasion, Chips had mercilessly yelped to the point where Dr. Brown said he could not think clearly, so Mrs. Larson had put him in the basement to wait while his littermates were examined.

"That's a good lad," she said as she locked him into a small wooden crate.

The place had not grown any more cheerful since Chips's last visit. It was still dark and cold, and it smelled of the mothballs Mrs. Larson scattered in the corners to keep away the mice. Occasionally, a delicious aroma would waft down the cellar stairs to his crate and make Chips's tummy grumble with delightful anticipation. Chips again thought of the word *home* and wagged his tail. But when no one appeared to take him back to the warm, sweet-smelling kitchen, he whined plaintively.

As time passed, Chips heard many different voices and footsteps above him. Sometimes he heard one of his brother or sister's joyful yips. Other times he heard the sound of children's clattering feet and laughing. The Larsons lived alone, but Chips knew the sound of young voices and footsteps. Mrs. Larson often invited the neighborhood children over to play with the puppies. She called it *puppy school,* and said that a dog that didn't like children would make a worthless pet. Now, as Chips listened to the patter of small running feet and the exuberant shouts and squeals that went with them, he longed to join them.

Hours passed, and still no one came to get the lonely puppy. Chips's throat grew hoarse from yipping, and it was all he could do to muster a pathetic whimper. Unfortunately, Mrs. Larson had been in such a hurry to get ready for her guests that she had neglected to put a bone or toy in his crate. Chips made do the best he could by shredding his red ribbon into threads and eating most of it. Gradually, his eyelids grew heavy, and in puppy fashion, he curled into a ball, tucked his round black nose into his soft fur, and fell into a deep sleep. When the door to the basement finally opened, the house had grown quiet and dark.

"The children insisted that we come back and see if there were any puppies left," said a pleasant-sounding woman's voice. Chips blinked into the shaft of light that spilled down the stairs. A woman with two young girls descended with Mrs. Larson.

"Gracious me," Mrs. Larson replied. "With all the people and the commotion I completely lost count of how many puppies were taken. I forgot about the big fellow in the basement. I charged five dollars for the others to cover Dr. Brown's veterinary bill, but you can have this one for free." She opened the door to Chips's wooden crate. "Oh dear," she exclaimed. "He's eaten his bow and gotten patches of red dye all over his lovely clean fur!"

The woman laughed. "What an unusual looking little dog. He has the longest ears I've ever seen. And just look at the size of those paws! They're as big as a wolf pup's!"

"I must admit he has a hearty appetite too," Mrs. Larson sighed. "I'm an honest woman and I wouldn't feel right if I didn't tell you that he eats as much as a full-grown dog. I wouldn't want you to think you were getting a bargain."

"Thank you for your honesty, Mrs. Larson. We'll keep that in mind. Isn't that right, children?" The woman spoke to the two young girls who were gently stroking Chips's velvety fur and taking turns kissing him on his downy soft nose.

"May I hold him?" the older girl asked as she reached for the squirming pup.

Chips immediately burrowed his nose into Gail's golden curls and licked her ear while she giggled.

"I want to hold him too!" her sister demanded, tugging on her mother's arm.

"You may have a turn, Nan," her mother answered. "But then baby John needs to meet him. If we decide to take this puppy with us, and I'm only saying *if*, we must be certain they'll be good friends too."

That's when Chips noticed a baby of about one year nestled on the mother's hip. The baby reached out and wound his chubby fingers tightly in the puppy's soft fur. Chips turned in Gail's arms and licked the baby's face. This made the baby giggle and let go.

"Look, Mother," Gail said. "They already like one another."

"So they do."

At that moment a man appeared at the top of the cellar stairs.

"Father, come see!" Gail shouted, and she passed the warm, furry bundle to her eager sister.

"The puppy and John are best friends now, so Mother says we can keep him," Nan added triumphantly.

Chips wriggled out of the little girl's arms onto the floor.

"I said no such thing," Nan's mother said as she hopelessly looked at the man. "I said, *IF*...."

Father only smiled.

Mrs. Larson, who had been listening intently,

coughed nervously.

"But wait...where did the puppy go, Mrs. Larson?" Gail asked.

"I haven't any idea, dear. He was here just a moment ago."

The grown-ups continued talking while the girls went upstairs to look for Chips.

Suddenly Gail called out from the dining room, "Mrs. Larson, come quickly!"

The three adults dashed up the stairs to find Chips standing in the middle of the dining table feasting on a platter of cookies.

"Good grief!" Mrs. Larson exclaimed. "That puppy's nothing but a bundle of mischief!" Yet no sooner did the big woman lung to grab the rambunctious dog than he leapt to the other side of the table and landed nose-deep in a large cheesecake.

At the sight of this the girls tumbled to the floor laughing. Their mother tried to hush them, but she couldn't keep a serious face either. In the end, everyone had a good laugh, including baby John, who waved his arms and babbled his approval.

"I can see this puppy will need a lot of civilizing. Wouldn't you agree, Mrs. Larson?" Mother gave the flustered Mrs. Larson a knowing wink. "But if the children promise to help train this little fellow, we'll take him home and try to turn him into a well-behaved dog."

"Yes!" Gail and Nan shouted at nearly same moment.

"You'd better think of a name for him so you can begin training him now," their father said as he grabbed

Chips, who was just about to scramble back onto the table, his eyes fixed on a platter of cheese.

"Let's call him 'Chips'," Nan said. "Mr. Chips because he has bits and chips of food stuck all over his fur!"

Everyone agreed.

"Do you hear that, Mr. Chips?" Gail said. "We're taking you home." Both girls cuddled their arms around the chubby puppy's neck.

That's when Chips understood that *home* meant children and his entire body wiggled with joy.

CHAPTER 2

SCHOOL RULES

"I wish the winter vacation didn't have to end," Gail moaned as she tossed off her bed quilt. "It's not fair that we have to go to school and John gets to stay home and play with Chips all day," Nan added.

Chips, having grown accustomed to the family's morning routine, meticulously groomed his front paws while he patiently waited for the girls to get dressed and have breakfast so they could begin another day of play with him. But as soon as they had eaten they grabbed their coats and book bags and ran out the front door, leaving him behind. Confused and puzzled, Chips mournfully whined and scratched at the door to follow them.

"I'm sorry, Chips," Mother said sympathetically. "But you can't go with them today."

★ ★ ★

As the weeks and months passed, Gail and Nan continued to leave each morning for the mysterious place called *school*. Chips tried to fill in the hours by chewing on bones, but he sometimes forgot himself and chewed Father's best dress shoes or Mother's favorite pillow. Sadly, these occurrences were met with sharp words and long hours exiled to the back yard. Life went on in this manner until one early spring day when a member of the village beautification committee paid Mother a visit.

"You mustn't forget to rotate the flower pots," said the stern-faced woman who sat drinking tea with Mother at the dining room table. "Young, tender plants must sun evenly all around or they will grow crooked."

"Don't worry, Mrs. Hale," Mother reassured her guest. "Your lilies will be safe and well-cared for at our home."

"I do hate to have to go out of town and leave them for a whole week. They will be the talk of the garden show next month. After all, they're my prized darlings— my babies!"

Chips, who was lying in a favorite corner of the dining room with his eyes closed and his head resting on his paws, had one ear tipped toward the women and the other turned in the direction of the stairs. He was eagerly anticipating John waking from his nap. He loved to race to the second floor ahead of Mother, stick his nose through the slats of John's crib, and tickle the little boy's toes with his tongue. Chips then let out a long, contented sigh that caught the visitor's attention.

"What breed of dog did you say he is?" Mrs. Hale

asked somewhat indifferently. Chips opened one eye halfway as he felt the gaze of both women turn toward him. "He's rather strange looking if you don't mind my saying so," the guest continued. "He doesn't look like any particular breed at all. Did you say he's a German shepherd? I never in my life saw a shepherd with slanted eyes and such ridiculously big ears."

Chips glanced up to return the cold look he spied in the visitor's eyes.

"Chips is only part shepherd," Mother answered politely. "His father was a husky and his mother was a shepherd-collie mix."

"Ah, you mean he's a mongrel," Mrs. Hale replied sourly. "I can always tell a dog that has no pedigree."

Chips's head shot up, and his top lip curled back to reveal pearly white puppy teeth. From somewhere down deep in his throat a small growl was born.

"How appalling! That mongrel is growling at me," Mrs. Hale gasped.

"Why, Chips," Mother said, frowning. "That's not polite behavior. I'm surprised at you. Growling at guests is never allowed in our home. You must stay in the yard if you can't behave yourself." With this Mother grabbed Chips by the collar and led him to the back door.

Yet no sooner had Mother whisked Chips out into the blustery spring day than he noticed a line of colorful clothes blowing on their neighbor's clothesline. The mask-faced puppy easily scrambled up and over the four-foot fence into the Rand's yard, and with one enormous leap, secured the end of a flowery sheet between his needle-sharp teeth.

It was the most fun he'd had since Gail and Nan had returned to school. Chips fought valiantly, lunging and snapping at the fluttering laundry until every piece lay torn and trampled on the ground. He was especially proud of his newfound growl and practiced it over and over again as he ripped and shredded each and every piece. Then he picked up a fragment of a man's shirt collar and trotted toward home to show his prize to Mother.

Chips was about to leap over the fence into his yard when he saw a woman running toward him. It was their neighbor, Mrs. Rand. She was waving a large yellow broom, and as she came within reach she whacked it down across his back. Chips had never been hit before, and he was so stunned it took a moment for the painful sting to register in his brain. Unfortunately, he paused a moment too long, and WHACK, the broom came down again, this time on his head. That was quite enough for Chips, and with a yelp he scrambled over the fence to safety.

Once back in his own yard, Chips noticed something he had not seen earlier. Lined up along the back shed were row upon row of little brown pots with slender green plant shoots sticking out of them. Being a dog, he was innately curious. Being a puppy meant that everything new had to be sniffed, poked, prodded, and even chewed. Within minutes Chips had successfully ripped all of Mrs. Hale's prized lilies out of their containers—roots and all.

He had just begun to gnaw on an old garden glove when he looked up to see Mother stomping toward him with a dark look on her face. Mrs. Rand was marching behind her, shaking a piece of torn laundry in her fist. Behind both of them, with a ferocious look on *her* face, was Mrs. Hale. She was wielding one of Mother's large iron frying pans over her head. Without hesitating, Chips made a beeline for the front yard, and with one great leap he cleared the gate and ran up the street as fast as his legs could carry him. He did not stop running until he was certain no one was following him.

It was the first time Chips had ever been outside of his yard by himself. Gail and Nan had always been with him and had watched over him. The world seemed different now that he was alone. Although he was certain that he had been on this street before, nothing looked or smelled familiar. For a brief moment Chips worried about finding his way back home. He sat down and softly whimpered.

Luckily, out of the corner of his eye, Chips saw a man dressed in a blue uniform slowly approaching him. The wind was blowing in Chips's direction so he carefully sniffed the air. He quickly recognized the scent and joyfully barked and wagged his tail. It was Mr. Green, the village mailman.

The big front door at home had a mail slot, and every afternoon Mr. Green would trudge to the door and slip the day's delivery through the opening. This created a wonderful game. Chips would race Mother to the entrance hall, and snatch up as many letters in his mouth as possible. Mother would then chase him through the house while John squealed and waved his arms to cheer him on.

"Hello, young fellow," Mr. Green greeted him.

"Aren't you the new pup that lives on Orchard Street? You've wandered pretty far from home. I don't have time to walk you back there now but maybe we can call your folks from a house along the way." Mr. Green smiled and patted his leg for Chips to follow him.

Chips wagged his tail and eagerly waited with keen anticipation. He could see the crisp white envelopes sticking out of the mailman's leather pouch. He crouched low on his haunches in the usual playful position and readied himself to pounce on a piece of mail. But then the mailman did something very strange: he turned around and walked away whistling to himself. Chips shrugged this off as a new kind of game, and happily trotted along behind him.

Chips and his companion steadily made their way up and down the sidewalks, and although Mr. Green knocked on the door of each and every house, no one could be found at home. Just when it seemed as though they were the only two in the neighborhood, an elderly woman opened her door to greet them.

"Good afternoon, Mrs. Ames," Mr. Green greeted her. "May I use your telephone to call this pup's family? It seems he slipped out of his yard, and now he's out on his own."

"Yes, of course," the woman said smiling down at Chips, who was busy watching a squirrel scampering through some nearby bushes.

"Stay here young fellow and I'll be back in a jiffy," Mr. Green instructed, giving Chips a pat on the head. "*Stay,*" he repeated in a firm but friendly voice and disappeared into the house.

No one had ever explained the meaning of the word *stay* to the busy puppy. Even if they had, it's doubtful he would have obeyed this command because at that moment what Chips heard in the distance beckoned to every bone and muscle in his roly-poly body. He heard the sound of children's shouts and whoops only a few short blocks away. It was recess time at Gail and Nan's school, and children were spilling out onto the playground. Chips did not hesitate for a moment. He turned and raced full steam toward the young voices.

Chips arrived amid welcoming screams and cheers. The children had never seen a dog in the schoolyard before, and he had never seen so many children at one time. It was a dream-come-true for everyone.

"Look, a dog!" a tall boy called out to his friends. Chips dashed into the center of the playground and made a full circle around the youngsters as if he were herding a group of young lambs. He raced around and around, nearly making himself dizzy.

"Let's catch him!" shouted a girl with long dark braids. Soon more than a dozen children were in hot pursuit of the playful puppy.

Chips easily outran each and every child. It was great fun. He dodged between them, running under slides and around swings. No matter how hard they tried, he was too fast for any of them to catch. One by one, the boys and girls stopped to regain their breath. Chips also stopped but it wasn't because he needed to rest. He was searching the crowd for the two children he loved most of all, Gail and Nan—but they were nowhere to be found.

All of a sudden a teacher opened the door of the school and shook a big brass bell. Everyone ran toward the door and filed inside. One boy had fallen and scraped his knee, and while the teacher examined it, the mask-faced puppy slipped through the school's entrance unnoticed.

The school was a big place. The seemingly endless hallways were lined with coats and book bags hanging on hooks. Chips passed room after room filled with children sitting and working at little wooden desks. Yet it wasn't long before his keen sense of smell led him to Gail's classroom. He was just about to enter the room when Gail's teacher marched out through the door and walked away in the opposite direction. Chips waited for a few moments until the woman had disappeared around a corner, then he proudly pranced into the room.

"Chips!" Gail exclaimed, barely able to believe her own eyes. "You came to school!" She gave him a big hug as her classmates gathered around to take their turn petting him.

Chips basked in the children's attention for several minutes. He licked their hands and faces and let them stroke his soft fur. He would have been content to remain that way for hours had he not caught the scent of something he had never smelled before.

On top of the teacher's desk was a small cage. Inside the cage was the teacher's pet hamster, *Fang*. Chips bounded up to the desk to investigate. He stretched his front paws up onto the desk and pawed at the enclosure. Fang glared and made a hissing sound. Chips pawed the cage again, but this time it toppled onto the

31

floor and its occupant popped out. Chips wagged his tail and barked excitedly. He wanted to play. The frightened hamster turned and scurried away. Chips happily chased the little fur ball up and down the aisles of desks while the children laughed and screamed.

"What's all of this commotion about?" the teacher asked as she entered the room just in time to see Fang dive under a radiator with the wolfish-looking dog in hot pursuit. She let out a terrified scream!

The school's head custodian escorted Chips to the principal's office at the end of a jump rope. Chips wagged his tail excitedly when Mother arrived to take him home, but Mother didn't speak to him or praise him for his adventures that day. Instead, she apologized to the principal and promised that Chips would never trespass on school property again.

That evening Mother and Father called a family meeting. It was decided that until Chips could act like a *responsible* and *civilized* dog, he would have to be chained to a tree when he was in the yard.

"Don't be sad, Mr. Chips," Gail said when she and Nan showed him to his favorite sleeping spot next to the fireplace. "Today was the most fun I've ever had at school!" Chips's almond-shaped eyes merrily twinkled in agreement.

CHAPTER 3

WATER RESCUE

By the time autumn arrived, Chips was nearly full-grown. In fact, he was so big that he could stand on his back legs, put his front paws on Father's shoulders, and look him squarely in the eyes.

"Do you know what the veterinarian, Dr. Brown, told me today?" Mother announced one night at dinner. "He said Chips weighs nearly 120 pounds! It's little wonder we can't seem to keep enough dog food in the house."

Chips was napping under the table, and pricked up his ears at the sound of his name.

"Ah, that reminds me," Father said. "Mrs. Rand stopped me on my way to work this morning. It seems when Chips broke free from his chain last week he got into her garbage cans and created quite a mess."

At that moment a bite-size piece of meatloaf tumbled off John's fork and hit Chips on the nose. He wagged his tail in appreciation and gave John a thank-you lick on his toes that made the boy squirm and giggle. Realizing what had happened, Gail and Nan each slipped some of their dinner under the table too.

"Children!" Mother scolded. "You're only making the situation worse by feeding Chips table treats. We must work together to make him a well-mannered dog."

"But Chips already *is* a well-mannered dog, Mother," Gail said. "He just wants to be free of that nasty old chain so he can run and play again."

"Gail has a good point," Father agreed. "Let's plan an outing to the beach this Saturday. It's still warm enough to swim, and Chips can have the run of the beach."

Having heard his name mentioned several times in the conversation, Chips thumped his tail with enthusiasm.

"The beach! Did you hear that, Mr. Chips? You've never been to the beach!" Gail exclaimed.

"Hurrah!" Nan shouted as John kicked his feet up and down and noisily banged his spoon on the table. Chips joined in with three deep barks.

★　★　★

Saturday morning arrived, and the family piled into the car with beach towels, sand toys, and a picnic hamper. Although the September day was warm enough to seem like summer, the beach was nearly deserted. Only a handful of striped umbrellas dotted the golden sand, and two white gulls called out to each other as they glided overhead.

During the trip in the hot car, Chips had worked up a tremendous thirst. The first thing he did when he got to the beach was race to the edge of the surf and take a gulp of seawater. The briny taste filled his mouth and throat, and sent him into spasms of sputtering and coughing.

"Poor Mr. Chips," Gail laughed, "He doesn't know the ocean is salty." She ran to get a thermos of fresh cold water while Nan patted the confused dog on the back.

As soon as Chips recovered he was ready to play. He ran back to the edge of the beach, snapping at waves and kicking up sand as he leapt out of reach of the foamy surf.

"Now that Chips knows the sea is not for drinking, I think he's enjoying his day at the beach," Mother said as she watched Gail and Nan chase the big dog along the shoreline.

After running in the hot sun the girls tired and decided to cool off in the ocean. As they waded in up to their waists, Chips stood by the water's edge, frantically barking.

"Just look at that nervous puppy," Mother remarked to Father. "I believe he's afraid to go into the water himself, so he's trying to get the girls to come back out. Since he's always so brave, I wonder why he's afraid of the water? He's even frightened of the bathtub at home." Mother thought to herself for a few moments. "I'll remember to ask Mrs. Larson, perhaps she knows the reason why."

"Whatever you think, dear," said Father, who was

busy reading his newspaper.

Finally, at Chips's insistence, the girls waded back to shore.

"What should we do now?" Nan asked.

"Let's build a sand fort."

"Good idea. Chips can be the guard dog and keep everyone else out—especially John." Nan couldn't forget how John gleefully smashed all of their sand castles on a trip to the beach earlier that summer.

The girls spent nearly an hour transporting buckets of wet sand from the shoreline to the site of their fortress. Chips dutifully trotted back and forth with them, all the while keeping a careful watch on their proximity to the water.

"If we build the fort any higher it'll collapse," Gail observed as she carefully surveyed their work. "Let's decorate it with shells."

The girls went to look for seashells while Chips happily trailed them. They had not gone far when they met a man and woman strolling along, arm in arm.

"That's a terrific looking dog you have," the man said, smiling.

"Is he friendly?" the woman asked, cautiously backing away.

"He's the friendliest dog in the world," Gail assured her. " He just looks big and scary."

"Don't worry," Nan added. "He doesn't bite."

The woman took another step back.

Being quick to sense fear in humans, Chips lay down on the sand to appear more approachable.

"Is that your red-and-white-checkered table cloth

and picnic basket?" Nan asked, pointing up the beach.

"Yes it is," the woman said proudly. "We're celebrating our wedding anniversary and I made a special lunch for us. This is the place where we first met."

The man and woman smiled at each other.

"Will you tell us about it?" Nan asked. She loved to hear the details about how her own parents had met.

The man and woman began to recount their story. While the children listened intently, Chips put his head down on his front paws and closed his eyes. The rays of the warm sun beating down on his thick fur and the sound of the waves rolling onto the shore nearly put him to sleep. All of a sudden, there was a change in the direction of the wind and with it, the faint aroma of something too good for any dog to ignore.

Chips lifted his head and carefully sniffed the air. His keen nose told him that a roast chicken was located in the vicinity of the checkered tablecloth he now noticed a short distance up the beach. While the girls and the couple laughed and talked, Chips casually got up and trotted over to investigate. He found the hen sitting on top of a picnic hamper, loosely covered in foil. He looked around. No other animal or person was waiting to claim his prize, so he picked the chicken out of its wrapping and holding it delicately in his mouth, walked up the beach to savor it alone.

The woman glanced up just in time to see their lunch being carried away. "Look! That horrible dog is stealing our chicken!"

No sooner did Chips hear the woman yell out than he knew he had done something terribly wrong. He was so frightened that he turned and ran along the beach with the cooked bird in his mouth.

Needless to say, when Mother heard about Chips's caper she was not pleased. The girls did their best to defend him, claiming that it was their fault for not watching him more closely. And even though Gail and Nan promised to pay for the couple's food out of their allowance money, Mother was determined to punish Chips as well.

"It's time for Chips to act like a grown-up dog. We'll have to take him home."

"But Mother, Chips didn't know the food belonged to anyone," Gail argued.

"It was sitting on the beach all by itself," Nan added. "If John had found it he probably would have taken a bite out of it too."

"Sorry girls, but I don't want to hear another word in Chips's defense. We're leaving the beach now and that's...."

Mother never finished her sentence. She looked twenty yards up the beach just in time to see John being knocked over by a large wave. He was so small that the undertow, although not strong, carried him out into the surf. Mother screamed. Father turned quickly but saw nothing, as John had disappeared in the frothy foam already. Suddenly a speeding dark object knocked into Father, sending him sprawling. Mother screamed again as the lightening-quick form reached the spot where she had last seen the boy and plunged into the surf.

Chips sputtered and gagged on the salt water as it washed over him, but one thought drove his entire being forward— to retrieve John. It was a desire born of an instinct so strong that all fear was erased from the determined dog's mind. Within seconds, Chips was struggling back toward the shore, carefully carrying the young child by the waist of his swim trunks. He laid the boy's limp body face down on the sand and nudged him gently. He could hear the boy's heart beating strongly.

Mother, Father, and the girls ran to John. Father folded the boy over his arms and squeezed under his ribs. John spit out the seawater that was lodged in his throat then let out a hearty cough.

"He's only swallowed a little water," Father said as he cradled John against his chest. "He should catch his breath in a minute. If he had been under the water any longer...." Father paused. The entire family had tears of relief running down their cheeks.

Meanwhile, Chips was feeling wet and miserable. He knew that John was not in danger any longer, and so he decided to look for a way to escape the salty ocean water that was making his entire body itch. The only relief he could find was to roll around in the sand.

That was what Chips was doing when the family turned to discover the source of strange moaning and groaning sounds. The giant dog was lying on his back, all four paws kicking into the air as he rolled and squirmed. When Chips finally stopped, he was covered in a thick layer of white sand and barely recognizable except for his big black nose and two long pointed ears sticking out from the top of his head. All tears turned to laughter.

Mother went to the sand-coated dog and put her

arms around his neck. "Chips, today you're a hero and you don't even know it. Your eyes and ears are better than a mother's or father's. You needn't stay chained in the yard any longer. And tonight you'll have the biggest roast beef bone I can find!"

Chips held his tail high in the air and pranced in a circle, joyfully barking.

Yet no amount of cajoling could get Chips to go back into the water to rinse off the sand that was caked to his body. Mother, however, didn't seem to mind the mess. She said that Chips could spend the rest of his days covered in dirt and dining from garbage cans and she wouldn't care one bit. Chips, she said, was the best and bravest dog that ever lived.

CHAPTER 4

MORE TROUBLE

As the months went by and a full year passed, Chips learned to create new games to amuse himself. Springtime was perfect for rolling around in the mud and splashing through rain puddles, and summer was full of trips to his favorite forest to track the trails of squirrels and rabbits, or to steal the occasional hot dog off the back yard grill. Autumn, Chips discovered, was a fine time for leaping into neatly arranged leaf piles and scattering the leaves into the wind. Not a few neighbors chased him out of their yards at the end of a rake. Still, Chips thought these pastimes were terrific fun, almost as much fun as chasing the village garbage truck. Chasing the rattling old dumpster had nearly become an Olympic event for Chips. It required speed, agility, and an uncanny sense of timing, all of which he was rapidly acquiring.

There was, however, one important rule to follow: Chips knew never to chase the truck on Orchard Street, the street where he lived. Aside from the fact that on his street the truck crept slowly from driveway to driveway and was no challenge for him, he was always within sight or earshot of Mother. Mother did *NOT* approve of chasing garbage trucks, and getting caught could land him on the back yard chain again. Chasing the giant dumpster on his street was out of the question, but on Manville Road it was another matter entirely.

Every Friday afternoon, when the children were safely home from school and snack time was over, Chips would politely scratch at the door to be let out. Once outside, he would bound to the end of his block and wait until his keen ears heard the truck's grinding gears shift as it picked up speed on Manville Road, a major thoroughfare in the town. At this hour, the sanitation vehicle was fully loaded and on its way to the local dump.

Villagers, who happened by, were astounded by what they witnessed: a wild-looking, mask-faced dog running, his slanted eyes glinting and his sharp fangs flashing through parted jaws. *Mad-dog, wolf,* and *monster* were just some of the names people called him. In truth, Chips was just having good old puppy fun. The object of his game was to beat the truck to the top of Manville Road before it turned north toward the dump, a distance of about one-quarter mile.

Chips loved everything about the truck. Being a dog, he loved the smell of days' old food and wet newspapers as he ran downwind of it. He liked the way the truck's gears sounded when they shifted, and he even liked the way in which the young man who stood on the back bumper yelled and angrily shook his fist at him as he drew closer.

Chips joyfully pursued this sport all through the fall, and always with great success, until one Friday in early December. On this particular day, he excused himself out the front door as usual and made his way to the end of the block to wait for his opponent to arrive. He raised his nose into the cold whipping wind. It was the kind of day his husky blood relished. A thin layer of ice was forming on the ground, and a light snow was falling. Chips eagerly licked the ice and felt the sharp air ruffle through his thick, dark fur. He was ready for an invigorating chase.

As soon as Chips heard the dumpster make its turn onto Manville, he pricked up his ears and set off at a fast gallop. But today there was something different about the truck. Instead of shifting gears and accelerating up the street, it sputtered and crawled at a snail's pace. Chips easily caught up with the creeping vehicle, and when he was barely a foot from it he locked his gaze with the young man who rode on the back. As usual, the man shook his fist and yelled at him, but because the truck was moving slowly, Chips heard the words as clearly as if they were having a conversation.

"Scram, you mangy mongrel. Get away from me or I'll give you a piece of this!" The man reached over into the back of the truck and pulled out a wooden baseball bat. He waved it threateningly and glared at Chips. "Come an inch closer and I'll whack you right between the eyes!"

Chips couldn't understand why the young man didn't share his appreciation of this harmless game. He also couldn't guess this human was so afraid of him that he often had nightmares about falling off the truck into the giant dog's jaws. In fact, the reason the man carried the bat was precisely because of Chips.

"I'll smash your skull!" the man shouted again and brandished the weapon over Chips's head.

If there was one thing Chips had learned in his brief life, it was that humans wielding brooms, rakes, and bats were very dangerous. Disheartened and disappointed, Chips decided to turn back toward home.

Yet, at that very moment, the truck began to slip and swerve on the ice. As it skidded so did Chips. To keep from sliding under the vehicle, he pushed with his back legs and lunged forward to reach his front paws and head up onto the back bumper. Dogs can't hold on well with their paws, but they can easily use their powerful jaws to gain a fast grip. Chips instinctively sank his teeth into the first object that provided a firm anchor. Unfortunately, his anchor was the young man's leg. With one ear-piercing scream the man brought the bat down, narrowly missing Chips's head. But as the man swung the bat he lost his balance, and both he and Chips tumbled onto the slippery road. They slid a good twenty feet before coming to a stop. Both man and dog lay on the ground dazed for several moments before the man began screaming.

"Help, help! I've been bitten! The mad wolf-dog bit me!"

Chips was stunned by the fall, but the man's screams scared him onto all four paws, and he raced home as fast as his legs could carry him over the slippery ice. He was in such a hurry to get to safety he didn't notice his friend, Mr. Green, the mailman, who had witnessed the entire unfortunate incident, and was running to help the injured man.

Chips felt relieved to be home. His old bone was waiting for him in the cozy spot next to the fireplace. The children fussed over him as usual and took turns stroking and brushing his thick fur. He completely forgot about his misadventure with the dumpster until later that evening when the doorbell rang.

As a dutiful guard dog, Chips always resorted to his most ferocious barking and growling when he heard a visitor at the door. This time was no exception. Generally, a caller at this late hour was a deliveryman with a business package for Father. Father was a lawyer, and he often received packages filled with official looking papers and documents. Mother would then say to the children: *Don't bother your father tonight; he has important work to do.* But on this night when Father opened the door Chips vaguely recognized one of the village's police officers standing in the shadows with a grim look on his face.

"Won't you come in, Officer Burke," Father said. "Is there some kind of problem?"

A dog can detect the slightest nuances in a human's voice, and Chips echoed Father's concerned tone with a low growl.

"It's okay, Chips," Father reassured him and took a secure hold of his collar.

But as policeman stepped into the house, Chips's

acute sense of smell detected the odor of the gun in his holster. He had never experienced the scent before and he naturally disliked it. The big dog lowered his head and growled more vehemently.

"What's gotten into you, Chips?" Father sounded annoyed. "I must apologize. He's usually a very friendly dog."

"That's not what I've heard," the officer said sternly as he glared down at Chips. "Mr. Charles Wilson of our village sanitation crew says your dog bit him today while he was on duty. Landed him in the hospital with six stitches in his leg. I'm going to have to take the dog down to the pound. They know what to do with vicious dogs down there."

"What's all this about Chips biting someone?" Mother asked as she dashed out of the kitchen. "Chips has been within my sight all day today...." Then Mother's voice faltered as she recalled letting him out alone after the children came home from school. She remembered how Chips scratched to go out every Friday afternoon at the same time. It was the same time she heard the garbage truck shift gears as it turned onto Manville Road. She looked down at Chips and her eyes turned as cold as steel.

Mother's look was all the punishment Chips needed. He had never felt so ashamed in his life.

After a lengthy conversation Mother and Father convinced Officer Burke that Chips was not a vicious dog, nor was he part wolf, as Charlie Wilson the sanitation man claimed. The policeman agreed that Chips could remain at home provided he did not go outside except when secured on a strong leash. He said Chips was *under house arrest*.

Chips spent the night and most of the next day brooding under the dining room table. Nothing strikes more deeply into a dog's heart than the disapproval of his family.

Chips's worst punishment of all was that Mother completely ignored him. She didn't call him to the kitchen for his dinner, she didn't stop occasionally from her work to tell him he was a *good dog*, and she didn't give him a kiss on the tip of his nose when she went upstairs to bed. Chips had never felt so miserable in his life.

The following day was Sunday, and as the family was getting ready for their afternoon meal, the doorbell rang again. Chips, worried that Officer Burke had returned, approached the door cautiously. This time, however, he heard the voice of their neighbor, Mr. Rand. Although Chips didn't particularly care for Mr. Rand, he was greatly relieved it wasn't the village policeman. What Chips couldn't detect was Mr. Rand brought news that would change his life and the lives of everyone the gentle dog knew, forever.

CHAPTER 5

DOGS FOR DEFENSE

"It's war!" Mr. Rand shouted as he tripped over the welcome mat in the foyer. "The Japanese bombed *Pearl Harbor*! They bomb.... bombed our *fleet*," he stuttered.

"Slow down, Ed," Father said, trying to calm his neighbor. "What's that you're saying?"

Mr. Rand gasped for air as he spoke. "Ann and I were listening to the radio when the show was interrupted to say that Japanese war planes bombed Pearl Harbor early this morning. Almost the entire fleet was hit! Can you believe it? This is war. It's war!" he repeated as he collapsed into Father's favorite chair next to the fireplace.

By this time Mother had entered the room and switched on the family radio. What Mr. Rand said was true: the American naval fleet at Pearl Harbor in Hawaii had been taken by surprise attack, and was almost completely destroyed by Japanese bomber planes. Mother, Father, and Mr. and Mrs. Rand spent the entire day sitting by the radio listening and speaking in hushed voices.

Mother got up many times to answer the telephone and each time Chips heard her repeat the same words. "Isn't this terrible! It means war!"

War....

Chips thought he had heard the word before, but he had never heard it repeated so often. He wondered what it meant. *Home, treat, beach, ball, bone.* Most of the words Chips knew meant good things, (*no* and *bad dog* being two unpleasant exceptions), and he tried to be hopeful about this new word too. But every time Mother or Father said *war* an uncomfortable feeling fluttered through his belly. Chips was, by nature, intuitive. He could *sense* things, and he almost always sensed the feelings in a human's heart, especially the humans he loved and cared about the most. Listening to Mother and Father's conversation left Chips with a sad and uneasy feeling in his own heart. It wasn't long before he was certain *war* was not a good thing.

The next several months passed in a flurry of activity. Mother and Father spent many hours discussing what their village would do to help on the *home front.* The children's school planned rummage sales, the village organized community raffles, and people bought *war bonds* to raise money. Everywhere, people tried to use less of what they really didn't need. Everyone made fewer car trips to conserve gasoline for the troops who were going to fight the war; there were fewer sweets to eat because sugar was difficult to import from Cuba and had to be *rationed*; and there were periodic *blackouts* at night when everyone in the village turned off their lights to practice in case there was an enemy *air raid*. Mother told the children not to complain about what they couldn't have, but the family often heard her sigh over not being able to buy silk stockings. The silk, she said, was needed to make parachutes for the paratroopers who would help win the war.

Throughout the winter the children remained interested in playing with Chips, but Mother and Father were often too busy to pay him much attention. In the evenings Chips would lie down in his usual spot next to Mother while she sewed and listened to the radio. Although Mother still gave him affectionate pats on the head, she was often distracted and would look up from her sewing to say things to Father like, *The Smith boy enlisted in the Navy*, or, *Did you hear, the Emerson twins are both going into the Army?* At these moments her voice would grow low and distant, and Chips could tell her heart was filled with sad thoughts. Then he would offer her his paw or rest his head on her knee with an empathetic sigh.

Mother and Father were especially interested in one particular radio program. They called it President Roosevelt's *fireside chats*. The entire family gathered around to listen to these broadcasts. Mother always reminded the children to be especially quiet because, as she explained, President Roosevelt had important things to say to his countrymen. She said the President had a difficult job to end the war and that all Americans must do their part to help.

Chips liked to listen to the reassuring sound of the man's voice on the radio. One evening the special talk was interrupted by the sound of barking. It was *Fala*, President Roosevelt's Scottish terrier. From that night on Chips listened carefully for the sound of the playful dog that was the President's faithful companion.

★ ★ ★

Spring came and the talk of war continued. One afternoon in April, Mother briskly strode into the kitchen with an armful of yellow daffodils. For the first time in months, she was happily whistling to herself.

"I'm so proud of you, Chips! You're going to help our country win this war!" she exclaimed and threw her arms around his neck.

Chips was puzzled at Mother's sudden exuberance, but he responded joyfully and wagged his tail at the excitement in her voice.

That evening, when the family was seated at the dinner table, Mother tapped her water glass with her spoon to get everyone's attention.

"I have the most wonderful news," she began. "I received a letter today from *Dogs for Defense*. It says our Mr. Chips qualifies to join the United States Army and they want him to begin training this summer!"

Chips, who was resting in his usual spot under the table, lifted his ears at the sound of his name.

"What's *Dogs for Defense*?" Gail asked cautiously.

"It's an organization that recruits dogs for the military," Father answered.

"Why?"

"Right now, the war is being fought far away in Europe and in the Pacific," Father explained. "But we still need to protect this country. The government is looking for dogs to perform *sentry and patrol work* here at home—to help guard our borders."

"You mean, Chips will be a soldier?" Nan asked.

"In a way, yes. Chips will be assigned to a soldier who will be called his *handler*. He'll live with his handler while he's in the Army, and he'll be trained to follow special directions and commands."

"But then Chips will be someone else's dog, won't he?" Gail felt a small lump growing in her throat.

"We aren't really giving Mr. Chips away, are we?" Nan joined in.

"He'll be perfectly safe," Mother said smiling. "And I'm certain he'll have great fun too. Chips is already a wonderful watch dog, but sometimes I think he's bored at home with just me and John to look after while you girls are at school."

"How long will he be away for?" Gail said with tears filling her eyes.

"I suppose until the war is over."

"Can we visit him once a week like Janie Rand visits her Granny?" Nan asked.

"I don't think so, dear."

"Why does Chips have to be the one to go?" Gail's face reddened. "I bet the Rands aren't giving away their dog to the Army!"

"We mustn't be selfish, Gail," Mother answered

firmly. "I'll miss Chips too, but we have friends and neighbors whose sons and daughters, sisters and brothers, and young fathers are going off to war. The least we can do is offer Chips's help. He's smart and strong. The recruiter for *Dogs for Defense* said he's exactly the kind of dog they're looking for."

"I don't care about any dumb war." Gail defiantly crossed her arms in front of her.

"Me either," Nan pouted.

"Chipsie no go," chimed in John.

Chips didn't understand why a conversation that included his name made his family angry, and he quietly whimpered.

Suddenly the doorbell rang and Chips jumped up with a howl. Father followed him to the front hallway.

The voice on the other side of the door gave Chips even more concern than his family's conversation. It was Charlie Wilson, the young man who rode on the back of the dumpster truck. But Chips then heard another voice. It was his friend, Mr. Green, the mailman. Upon recognizing one of his favorite people, Chips eagerly wagged his tail and pawed for Father to open the door.

"I wanted to apologize before I left town," Charlie said as soon as he saw Father. "Jim here witnessed the whole incident with your dog the day he bit me—well, now that I've talked to Jim, accidentally bit me would be a better way to put it, I reckon."

"What Charlie's trying to say is he knows Chips meant no harm, and that the bite was only an accident," Mr. Green explained. "We wanted to be sure you knew it wasn't Chips's fault before we left for training camp."

"Training camp?" Mother asked as she greeted the young men at the door.

"That's right," Mr. Green continued proudly. "Charlie and I enlisted in the Army. We both got called to report for duty next week."

"Chips is going into the Army too," Gail said softly.

"Why, Chips, you are a brave one!" Mr. Green said with a wide grin. "Big Chips is enlisting too. Well, how do you like that?"

"The war should be over in six months once we get in there—right, Jim?" Charlie said as he gave his friend a knowing jab in the ribs. "Us *Yanks* will end it fast. We'll teach those *Axis powers* a lesson or two!"

Chips, who had been listening intently to the conversation didn't comprehend what his humans were saying. He only knew his name had suddenly become entwined with the word *war* and this made him feel uneasy.

★ ★ ★

What neither Chips nor the others knew was that the Second World War, as it had come to be called, would last longer than six more months. It would, in fact, drag on for three more years. The military would not only use dogs to safeguard the country's borders, but the biggest and smartest dogs would be sent overseas to work side by side with soldiers in some of the deadliest combat the world had ever known. And Chips would be in the first group to go.

CHAPTER 6

PRIVATE CHIPS
REPORTS FOR ACTIVE DUTY

"Time for breakfast!" Mother called from the kitchen. Chips yawned and stretched. He had been dreaming about the Rands' new garbage can with its puppy-proof lid. In his dream, however, Mrs. Rand had accidentally left the can open, and it was filled with bacon, still warm and smoking from the frying pan. Chips's mouth had watered in his sleep.

However, no sooner was he fully awake than he realized Mother was frying bacon in the kitchen. He also thought he detected the sweet aroma of maple syrup, which could only mean one thing: pancakes! Mother often gave him the first pancake from the grill, and he trotted into the kitchen to be of assistance.

It was Sunday, Chips's favorite day of the week: the

day when the entire family was at home. It was also summertime—a time when weekends were full of adventures. Chips quickly spotted two garden shovels and a rake Father had placed by the back door the night before. A day of gardening meant there would be sticks to chew, dirt to dig, and the children were certain to play plenty of games of chase and fetch. Yet when the girls came into the kitchen for breakfast they looked sad and gloomy. Chips felt his exuberant Sunday spirits crumble.

"Does Chips have to leave for the Army today?" Gail asked. "Why can't we wait a few more months? The war should be over by then. Both you and Father said the war would be over soon."

At the sound of his name, Chips stopped licking the maple syrup from John's fingers. It was that word *war* again. He had come to dislike this word most of all.

"But Father says we're planting our *victory garden* today," Gail continued. "My teacher says a victory garden is the perfect way to contribute on the home front. Why isn't that good enough?"

Mother gave Gail a stern look.

"Chipsie's going bye-bye," John said sadly and gently patted the big dog on the nose.

At that moment, Father walked into the kitchen. When Mother glanced up, Chips was certain he glimpsed a tear in her eye.

"Looks like we have a sunny day to begin planting," Father said, giving Mother a reassuring wink. "It's too late in the summer to start tomatoes and beans, but I think we can manage to grow squash and pumpkins by

October."

"I hate squash," Gail snapped.

"Me too," added Nan.

"Well, we'll have great pumpkins for jack-o-lanterns this Halloween," Father said, forcing a smile.

Gail's face grew stormy. "Halloween won't be any fun this year without Chips."

Mother and Father looked at each other but said nothing. Gail and Nan were silent too. Only John continued to prattle while swinging his feet back and forth in his chair.

Chips, sensing his family's sadness, put his head on his front paws and let out a long sigh.

"If this is Chips's last day at home, then I think we should do something special with him," Gail finally announced, breaking the silence.

"I know," Nan said. "Let's take Chips to the forest up near the lake. It's his favorite place to play and explore."

"Yes, our victory garden can wait," Father agreed, and gave Chips the usual scratch behind his ears.

★   ★   ★

It was a warm day in late summer, but the forest was shaded with leafy oak and elm trees. Chips loved to run free through the dappled sunlight, following the scent of squirrels and rabbits and other woodland creatures. Sometimes he stopped to help Gail and Nan hunt for salamanders. When he had his fill of romping, he lay down and buried his nose in a cluster of cool ferns with the children nestled close to him.

"When Chips comes back from the war this is the first place we'll visit," Gail said.

"That will be very soon, won't it?" Nan looked at her sister for reassurance.

"Yes, but this is a special day and we shouldn't make Chips feel sad. Instead, let's think of something fun to tell him."

"Like what?"

"Well," Gail thought for a moment, "I saw Mrs. Wilson in the grocery store last week and I heard her tell Mother that she bakes cookies and sends them to Charlie. We can do the same thing for Chips."

Chips nuzzled his big black nose close to Gail's face and gave her a lick on her cheek and then did the same to Nan."

"I think he knows exactly what we're telling him," Nan said.

"Of course he does, silly. Mr. Chips understands everything."

★ ★ ★

It was early evening when the soldiers finally arrived to take Chips away. Two young men, not much older than Mr. Green and Charlie Wilson and dressed in tan-colored uniforms appeared at the door. They introduced themselves as Sergeant Hart and Private Davis.

Chips thought they had friendly faces, and when they spoke to Mother they sounded gentle and kind. He cautiously sniffed their legs and feet. They both wore highly polished black boots that smelled like Father's best Sunday shoes. A dog can tell a lot about a human just by sniffing. Chips immediately knew both men were strong and sincere. Yet more importantly to him, he knew they were fond of dogs.

"We're here to collect *K-9* Chips for military service," the soldier called Sergeant Hart said.

Nan looked so sad the other soldier added: "Don't worry, Miss, we'll take extra good care of your dog."

"Where are you taking him?" Gail demanded and pushed past Mother to stand protectively between the men and Chips.

"We're here to escort him to the *War Dog Training Center* in Front Royal, Virginia," answered the sergeant in a respectful but firm voice. "First he'll be examined by our veterinary staff and then he'll be placed in *quarantine.*"

"What's quarantine?"

"That's when we keep a dog in isolation until we know he's healthy and can be with the other K-9's."

"But we play with Chips every day and he hasn't made us sick," Nan piped in.

"Dogs can have diseases only other dogs can catch," Mother explained.

"He'll begin his basic training in *boot camp*," the sergeant continued. "When he's finished with training, he'll be assigned to a *war dog platoon.*"

"What's a *platoon*?" Gail wanted to know.

"That's the group of soldiers he'll be assigned to work with when he's sent out on his missions."

"Missions? Where?"

"Don't worry, girls," Mother interjected. "Our Chips will be stationed somewhere safe in the United States. Isn't that right, Sergeant Hart?" She smiled confidently at the soldier as she spoke, but the sergeant was busy directing his assistant, Private Davis, to put a muzzle and leash on Chips and didn't hear her. "Oh, there's no need to restrain Chips with a *muzzle*," Mother continued. "He's as gentle as a lamb."

"Sorry Ma'am, Army rules and regulations," Private Davis said apologetically.

Chips shook his head and struggled against the unfamiliar feel of the muzzle as it rubbed across his soft nose. Except during the days when he had been tied in the backyard, he had rarely been restrained.

The young private tried to reassure Chips and gently spoke to him as he adjusted the leather straps. Chips could see and hear the soldier's kindness, but he didn't understand why he was wrapping the uncomfortable restraint over his head. Aside from harmlessly taking a piece of leftover bacon from the kitchen table, Chips could think of nothing else he had done wrong that day.

"We must be going now if we're going to catch our train out of New York to Front Royal," the sergeant said. "It's a mighty long trip," he added.

"Yes, of course," Mother agreed. "Say goodbye, girls, and let the soldiers be on their way."

Gail and Nan barely had time to hug Chips good-bye before the men turned and whisked him out the door and into their car.

Chips looked out of the car's rear window and

watched Mother, Father, the girls, and John wave to him from the front yard until the car turned out of Orchard Street and they disappeared from sight.

★　★　★

Chips had never been on a train before. And although he grew accustomed to the rattling sounds it made as it moved along the tracks, and the screeching sound of the brakes when it stopped to board and unload passengers, he couldn't stop feeling homesick. In his mind's eye, Chips saw his family. He sniffed the air and listened carefully but he had lost all trace of them. He whined softly to himself. Gradually, the movement of the train and the voices of the soldiers enveloped him in a light sleep. When Chips woke up it was nearly dawn.

"Next stop is Front Royal, Virginia," announced the train conductor.

"This is where we get off, Chips," Private Davis said, giving a gentle tug to his leash.

CHAPTER 7

QUARANTINE

Front Royal was a sleepy little town nestled in the foothills of the Shenandoah Mountains. Not since 1862, when Confederate and Union troops chased each other through the streets engaged in mortal combat, had people seen so much excitement. Now, with the new *War Dog Training Center,* the town had suddenly found itself once again bustling with soldiers and war preparations.

Sergeant Hart and Private Davis led Chips through the crowded platform. The station was swarming with men and a few women dressed in uniforms. The men wore shiny black boots that clicked on the pavement as they walked. Chips stayed close to the legs of his two escorts and they occasionally urged him on with *come boy* or *hurry up boy.* They stopped only once to talk with a group of soldiers. While they exchanged Army gossip, Chips spotted a boy of about ten years old walking with his mother. Excited to see a possible playmate, he eagerly wagged his tail and let out two wistful barks as best he could, for the muzzle was still securely fastened around his head.

"Look at the giant dog!" exclaimed the boy and began pulling his mother toward Chips.

"Heavens, Frankie, don't go near him. You know you're not supposed to pet *war dogs*. They can be very dangerous, and that one looks vicious!" With these words the mother hurried the child away. Chips's tail drooped as he watched the boy being pulled in the opposite direction, and he reluctantly turned and followed his own escorts to a waiting car.

The army car, or 'jeep' as the soldiers called it, was not like any vehicle Chips had ridden in before. It looked like a tin box on wheels with a canvas roof over it. Chips was instructed to sit in a small space behind the back seat. Sergeant Hart sat in the front next to the driver, and Private Davis sat behind him. The jeep bolted to a start, and Chips bounced from left to right until his insides shook as it bumped and rattled down a badly rutted road.

"We'll be arriving at the *post* any minute now," the driver said.

Sergeant Hart nodded to Private Davis, "Just in time for breakfast in the *mess hall.*"

"Did you hear that, Chips?" Private Davis called back to the big dog as they rattled along. "We have one of the best cooks in the United States Army. We get sausage, ham, and bacon almost every morning."

Chips, who had not eaten anything except for a few tidbits on the train, wagged his tail and let out two sharp barks of approval at these familiar and welcomed words.

"I'm afraid those *rations* are off limits to our new *recruit,*" Sergeant Hart interrupted. "Chips has to report directly to the veterinary unit for three weeks of quarantine. They'll have K-9 rations for him there."

Private Davis reached over the back of his seat and scratched Chips under his chin. "Don't worry, old boy. It won't be so bad. Sergeant Hart and I'll come by and see you every day. We're buddies now."

Chips wagged his tail. He liked the way the soldiers spoke to him as if he were one of them.

"Here we are," announced the driver. "The Front Royal War Dog Training Center. Good luck in boot camp, Chips," he added as he opened the jeep's door for the big dog to jump out.

"Take Chips over to the *infirmary* and sign him in," Sergeant Hart directed.

"Yes, sir," Private Davis replied and saluted his superior officer.

The Army post was comprised of long white buildings with black peaked roofs neatly and uniformly arranged in rows like a checkerboard. In the middle of the camp was an open grassy area, and in the center of the grass stood a tall flagpole.

"Once you're out of quarantine you'll be living beside one of these *barracks,*" Private Davis explained.

It was then Chips noticed the buildings had rows of little wooden doghouses lined up next to them. He sniffed the air and clearly detected the scent of other canines, but there were none in sight.

The two continued to walk past rows of barracks and doghouses until they came to a *Quonset hut* with a large red cross painted on the door. It was the K-9 infirmary. Chips immediately recognized the same medicinal odors as those in Doctor Brown's veterinary office back home, and he instinctively hesitated. The last time he visited his least favorite place he had not been pleased. Mother said the white-coated man was the nicest animal doctor in town, but she had been wrong. Not only had Doctor Brown cleaned Chips's ears with strong smelling alcohol swabs and poked and prodded him in the belly with a cold metal stethoscope, he had also given him two vaccination shots that hurt so badly he had not been able to sit comfortably for days. Chips refused to be fooled again.

"Come along and be a good dog," Private Davis urged, tugging on Chips's leash.

Chips dug his paws into the dirt and refused to budge.

"You'll like our Captain Hill. He's the best dog doctor in the Army." But try as he might, Private Davis, who was as big and strong as a soldier can be, could not get Chips to move.

Just then an older gentleman wearing a uniform with colorful stripes and glistening gold pins rounded the corner and nearly collided into both of them. "What's all this, Private?" the man said looking annoyed. "Why isn't this K-9 out with the other dogs? Is he sick?"

Private Davis immediately loosened his grip on the leash, stood at attention, and saluted his superior officer. "Colonel, sir, Private Davis and K-9 Chips reporting to quarantine, sir."

As soon as the young soldier released his grip on Chips's leash the new recruit seized the opportunity and bolted, nearly knocking the colonel to the ground.

"Stop that dog!" the colonel shouted as Chips galloped away with his leash dragging behind him toward an open field and freedom. "I'll have none of these shenanigans in my camp, and I won't stand for K-9's going *AWOL!*"

"Yes, sir, right away, sir," Private Davis said, saluting backwards as he ran after the four-legged renegade.

Chips had no trouble out-running his new friend, but he quickly discovered that the post was completely surrounded by a high wire fence. He raced along the base of the enclosure, but try as he might he couldn't find a way out. Meanwhile, a dozen soldiers had heard the colonel's shouts and come running from all sides.

But what stopped Chips dead in his tracks was not the threat of the advancing soldiers but the sight of more than one hundred dogs walking in single file less than fifty yards from where he stood. The K-9's were returning from their morning field exercises. Chips had never before seen so many dogs at one time!

They were mostly big dogs: German shepherds, Belgium sheepdogs, collies, Siberian huskies, bloodhounds, Airedales, Doberman pinschers, and mixes of these breeds, each walking calmly and obediently next to a soldier. All, that is, except for one who repeatedly stepped out of the neat single file line.

"Remove your K-9 from the others if he can't obey

commands," shouted a big fleshy-faced man who seemed to be in charge of the parade of men and dogs.

"Jake can't help it, sir," his soft-spoken, redheaded handler apologized. "He gets nervous when other dogs follow too closely behind us." The lanky black and gray mix-breed called Jake nervously turned to look at an oversized German shepherd who was glaring at him with eyes narrowed to slits. "Jake was bitten last week, and he's afraid it's going to happen again."

"That's not my problem, soldier. Either keep your recruit in line or take him back to the kennel. We don't have time for scared, sissy dogs. If he can't *cut-the-mustard* he doesn't belong in the Army!"

Chips didn't like the tone in the burly man's voice. He lowered his head and hunched up his shoulders to show his disapproval. Then he watched as Jake returned to the line with his handler. The nervous dog continued to glance over his shoulder at the steely-eyed shepherd who could easily have taken a bite out of his tail, had he been so inclined.

"I hope you were paying attention to that little incident," the colonel said when Private Davis walked Chips back to him. "Our K-9 recruits must follow orders at all times." He looked down and surveyed Chips from nose to tail. "He's an odd-looking example of his species, but I can see he's strong and fast."

"Yes, sir, Chips is quite a fellow," Private Davis replied and gave the giant dog a pat on the head.

"*Chips*, you say. I'll remember that name. But you remember, Private, he's worth nothing to the Army if he's not properly trained."

"Yes, sir."

The colonel paused to remove a bright gold watch from his waist pocket and check the time. Then he turned on his heel and disappeared around the corner of the building, leaving Private Davis to salute the air.

"You heard the colonel's orders, Chips," the young soldier said and dragged the still unwilling recruit into the veterinary office.

★   ★   ★

"Well, well, what do we have here?" a man wearing a white coat approached them. His eyes smiled as he peered at Chips and Private Davis over the top of round, wire-rimmed spectacles.

"K-9 Chips reporting to quarantine, Captain," Private Davis saluted the doctor.

Chips could see the man wore the same tan-colored uniform under his white doctor's coat as the other soldiers.

Before Chips had a chance to react, the doctor knowingly ran his hands along his shoulders and ribs, peered into his ears, and pulled back his lips to examine his teeth and gums. "Chips looks to be in good health, Private."

"Thank you, sir."

Then Captain Hill looked into Chips's eyes and spoke to him, "Would you like water, boy?"

Hearing the word *water*, Chips realized how thirsty he was and immediately felt friendlier toward this doctor. He wagged his tail and twitched his ears to express his interest.

"You see, Private, Chips is letting us know he needs a drink. It's what we mean when we say you have to be observant and *read the dogs*. A dog communicates with his body as well as his barks."

"Yes, sir, Chips sure is a smart dog," Private Davis answered proudly.

"I'm sure he is," smiled the captain. "You can leave him with us now. We'll keep him isolated in quarantine for three weeks. When we're certain he's as healthy as he looks we'll release him to join the other dogs." Captain Hill took Chips's leash from Private Davis and handed it over to a young officer who also wore a white coat over his uniform. "My lieutenant will make certain Chips has everything he needs. Don't worry, Private, your pal is in good hands."

Chips sadly watched his new friend disappear out the door, and then he followed the lieutenant into another room where he was placed in a large wooden crate. It was empty except for a bowl of fresh water. Chips immediately took a long drink, and then lay down to contemplate his new surroundings.

There were several other crates lined up along the opposite wall from his. Chips sniffed the air and immediately knew two were occupied. He let out a dog-style whine. A moment later, a deep bark came from one of the other crates. Then there was another bark from the opposite end of the room. This second one was higher pitched and sweeter sounding. Chips barked back and patiently waited for a reply, but the mysterious dogs refused to answer. Too exhausted from his long journey to investigate further, he closed his eyes. Gradually, Chips began to drift into a light sleep as he listened to Captain Hill and the lieutenant talking in the next room.

"Chips's records say he's a shepherd-husky-collie mix, and weighs 120 pounds," the captain said, placing the new file on his desk.

"That's a powerful mix of breeds, sir," remarked the lieutenant who was new to the infirmary.

"Yes, I can see why the Army was so interested to have him. He has no doubt inherited strength and speed from his husky ancestors. They're capable of traveling great distances without tiring." Then the captain hesitated and shook his head. "But he may also be imbued with their independent nature."

"Sounds like that could be a problem in the Army."

"A husky's more apt to follow his own natural instinct than to blindly obey a human's command. But Chips is also part shepherd. Shepherds are known for their loyalty and intelligence, yet they can be cautious and wary of strangers—good characteristics for any war dog."

"And what about his collie lineage?"

Here Captain Hill paused and smiled. "I've never met a collie that wasn't loyal and kind. The English farmers who have used them for centuries to herd sheep and cattle tell stories about their uncanny sense of intuition. They claim these dogs can read a man's mind and know the truth in his heart."

"Did you read the note attached to Chips's file?" the lieutenant asked, changing the subject. "It says his favorite food is roast beef. I don't suppose he'll be getting much of that around here. Looks like it was written in a woman's handwriting. I'll bet the mother of the family wrote it."

At the mention of the word *Mother*, Chips's eyes opened wide and his ears alerted forward. He'd been so preoccupied observing and sniffing his new surroundings—not to mention exhausted from his tiring journey—he hadn't thought about *home* since his train ride. Now, as he rested alone in the wooden crate he listened intently for Mother's voice and the children's laughter or footsteps, but try as he might he couldn't hear them, and he softly whimpered.

"You can always tell which dogs have come from loving homes," the captain continued. "I don't simply mean by their good health and condition, but in the way they carry themselves: by their stature. Chips has been well- loved. It shows in the proud way he stands and holds his head high. However, some of these donated dogs come from families who just want to be rid of them. Take that dog, Jake, who was quarantined last month. If we hadn't doubled his feedings he never would've passed inspection. It's easy to see he never had the proper care and attention a dog deserves."

"At least the Army will feed Jake and treat him properly."

"Yes," the captain agreed. "Yet, when the war ends, I can't help but wonder what will happen to a dog like Jake?"

★   ★   ★

Over the next two weeks, Chips remained in isolation. The doctors fed and played fetch with him behind the infirmary. They even took him for short walks around the building. His new friends, Sergeant Hart and Private Davis, kept their promise and stopped by every day to say a few kind words to him, but Chips was lonely...very lonely. As far as he was concerned, life in the Army was dull and quiet. He was homesick. He missed his grassy yard to run in, he missed greeting the children when they came home from school, he even missed his neighbor, Mrs. Rand, and the way she yelled at him every time he foraged through her garbage pails! But most of all Chips missed having a job to do: he missed guarding and watching over his family.

Occasionally, Chips caught glimpses of the two other quarantined recruits through the slats in his crate as they were led out for exercise, but they were never allowed to play together. The dog with the deep bark was called Pal. He was a big and muscular shepherd mix. The other one, Mena, was also a mixed-breed, but she was fine-boned and had a sweet, gentle expression. Although Chips enjoyed watching the comings and goings of these two dogs, he desperately wanted to romp with them and he scratched and barked to be set free whenever they were led past him.

"Sorry, old boy," the lieutenant said one day when Chips pawed at his crate as Pal went out for his early morning walk. "Army regulations say three weeks of quarantine for all recruits. Just a few more days and you'll be on your way to boot camp." The lieutenant was about to leave through the front office when he suddenly stopped and tied Pal to the door handle. "Hold on, fellow, I forgot to give Chips his water." He opened Chips's crate to refill his dish. Pal barked impatiently as he did so, and the lieutenant hurriedly shut the crate door to leave with the eager dog.

Chips took a drink and circled around his space the way dogs do before lying down. That's when he noticed an opening in the wooden slats he had never seen before. He sniffed to investigate and discovered the door to his crate was left ajar. He gave it a push with his nose and it opened instantly. Chips stepped out and looked around. Captain Hill was away from the office, and the lieutenant was still out walking Pal. Chips quietly approached the screen door that led out to the back of the building.

Chips was about to shoulder the door open when he saw Mena eyeing him from her crate. He approached and they pressed their noses in a crack between the slats of the wooden box in dog-style greeting. Chips liked Mena immediately and wagged his tail as an invitation for her to join him. Mena scratched at the door of her enclosure but it wouldn't budge. She barked plaintively. Suddenly Chips heard the lieutenant and Pal enter the front office. He knew he had to make a quick exit if he was going to escape. Chips gave Mena's crate a nudge with his nose to say good-bye, turned, and bolted out the back door to freedom.

It was a warm and breezy day, and Chips enjoyed the way the wind blew into his face as he ran. He stretched his legs as he gathered speed and headed in a northerly direction toward home. Chips soon reached the high wire fence he had encountered on his first morning on the post. He followed the fence, looking for a gap large enough to squeeze his body through. At last he found an open gate. Amazingly, it was wide enough for a small truck to pass through. Chips stopped and sniffed the ground. He readily detected the scent of both men and dogs, and he immediately followed their trail.

Chips moved at a gentle loping run across meadows and through wooded glens for what seemed like several miles. He had just stopped to take a drink from a cool, clear stream when he heard loud crackling and popping sounds in the distance. The rumbling reminded him of the firecrackers he sometimes heard coming from the village park at home on hot summer nights. Chips stopped to sniff the air, but he was upwind of the sound and could not key in on a scent. He continued to move closer to the source of the popping noise. As he grew closer the banging intensified until it became loud blasts.

Suddenly Chips caught the distinctive odor of something he had smelled before, something that stirred unpleasant memories. He made his way through a cluster of trees and across a field toward a big hill in the direction of the scent. But as Chips reached the rise on the hill what he saw below made him freeze in his tracks.

More than one hundred men and dogs were crawling on their bellies across a large field wearing strange masks over their faces! Across the rise from where Chips stood, on another hillside, soldiers were firing *howitzers* over the heads of these creeping soldiers and canines. *Shells* from the small cannons created thick clouds of smoke. Chips remembered the familiar smell of Officer

Burke's gun when he had come to the house to take him to the dog pound for accidentally biting Charlie Wilson. This time the odor stung his eyes and throat, and he gagged and choked on the sharp fumes.

All at once, someone grabbed Chips from behind, wrestled him to the turf, and strapped one of the masks over his head. Chips could barely see or breathe with the odd contraption wrapped around his eyes and muzzle. He struggled to escape but the large man who had tackled him kept his shoulders pinned to the ground.

"Stay down, you crazy critter," the man's voice shouted in his ear. "Are you trying to get both our heads blown off?"

Chips detected more concern than anger in the voice, and he slowly relaxed his body under the man's weight. As the explosions continued he gradually grew accustomed to breathing with the awkward shield over his face. It had two holes for his eyes and his nose fit neatly into a round-shaped canister. Although he was uncomfortable, Chips no longer choked on the smoke filled air. After what seemed like an hour but was in reality only a few minutes, the deafening explosions stopped.

"What's all this about?" an older man shouted as he was chauffeured toward them in an open jeep.

Chips quickly recognized the colonel he had met his first day on the post.

"I found this dog wandering around with no *gas mask* on," the soldier who had grabbed him explained.

"And no proper *working collar* either, I see," the colonel added. "These are serious war exercises, soldiers, not fun and games. Who belongs to this K-9?" The colonel looked out over the men but no one came forward to claim Chips. "Well, speak up, or there will be worse consequences to face." He looked back down at the confused dog. "I know I've met this mutt before. A big silly-looking dog...." That's when the colonel recalled his first encounter with Chips and shook his head.

Fortunately, at that moment, Sergeant Hart appeared. "Chips!" he exclaimed.

"I believe this K-9 is part of your outfit!" the irate colonel bellowed.

"He's supposed to be in quarantine, sir. I can't imagine how he escaped..."

The colonel scowled, "Soldiers, meet K-9 Chips. I suspect he's a heap more trouble than he's worth. In fact, I think he's so troublesome, I wouldn't mind having him wreak a little havoc on the enemy. I have plans for you, Chips, big plans!" With these words the officer abruptly turned on his heel, got into his jeep, and ordered his driver to speed away, leaving everyone including the bewildered dog, staring after him.

CHAPTER 8

BOOT CAMP

The next few days progressed slowly. Captain Hill and the lieutenant were too busy to spend time with Chips, and both Pal and Mena had been released from quarantine. Even though the three dogs hadn't been allowed to play together, Chips felt lonelier knowing they were gone.

Then, one morning, Private Davis appeared at the infirmary with a wide grin on his face.

"I have orders for Chips to report to boot camp," he said. "The colonel just announced that Sergeant Hart has been put in charge of the first K-9 platoon being sent overseas. The colonel wants to be sure Chips is with them. He says no *homeland security* post is good enough for Chips. He wants him in the thick of it: where the action is. Can you believe it, Captain? Chips is going to be with the very first group of dogs to go to war!"

Chips wagged his tail at all of the excitement as he cocked his head to one side and tried to comprehend what his friend was saying.

"He's in perfect health," Captain Hill agreed. "I see no reason why he can't begin his training today." He turned and spoke to the curious dog while patting him reassuringly on his head. "You're going to be a fine soldier, Chips. Sergeant Hart is a good leader; although lieutenants usually command platoons, the colonel has put him in charge. And I hear you've been assigned to a wonderful *handler*. Isn't that right, Private Davis?"

"Yes, sir. Chips is going to work with Private John Rowell. I'm taking him to meet Rowell now."

"Chips is lucky. Not only is Rowell a smart soldier but he understands dogs." The captain knelt down next to Chips and looked him squarely in the eye. "You're going to get a new master, boy. Private Rowell will be the only one allowed to look after you. He'll be the only one permitted to feed, groom, and play with you. It won't be because we don't want to do these things but because these are the rules. It's important that you learn to depend only on him. It's important for both your safety and the safety of your men."

Chips affectionately licked the young doctor's hand.

Private Davis took Chips by jeep to a part of the Army post he'd never seen before. It was a big open field. In the middle of the field stood a circle of twenty men with dogs on leashes. Two soldiers approached them.

Chips immediately recognized Sergeant Hart and

wagged his tail in anticipation of seeing his friend. The other man was a stranger. He was young-looking, with short-cropped blonde hair, and he carried a metal *choke collar* in his hand.

"Private Rowell, meet your K-9 partner," Sergeant Hart said.

"So this is Mr. Chips," the soldier spoke with a slight southern accent. "He's a fine-looking dog, all right. A big fellow too," he added and slipped the chain collar over Chips's head. "After you learn all of your commands you'll get a leather *working collar,* but for now you must wear this one."

Then Rowell led Chips to the training circle with the other men and dogs. Chips couldn't believe his good luck when he saw Pal and Mena, but when he excitedly wagged his tail and tried to run to them, Private Rowell pulled him back. Strangely, both Pal and Mena turned away and looked up at their respective handlers.

"No, Chips," Rowell said gently but firmly. "In the Army we never *fall out of line* unless we're given the order to do so. It'll take time, but you're a smart one. I can tell." Then the private told Chips to *heel* at his left side, and they walked around in a circle with the other dogs.

Although Chips caught several quick glances from both Pal and Mena, he was keenly aware that no sniffing, barking, or fraternizing of any sort was allowed. This was difficult for a friendly, outgoing dog like Chips, but he obeyed Private Rowell. There was something kind yet determined about the young soldier that made Chips eager to please him.

★　★　★

Captain Hill had been right. In the weeks that followed Private Rowell was the only soldier who touched or spoke to Chips directly. He and Rowell spent nearly every minute of every day together in training. At night, Chips slept in one of the little doghouses outside the long white barrack where Rowell slept. They got up every morning when the bugler played *reveille,* and stood side-by-side at attention when the country's flag was raised. They jogged two miles before breakfast, which for Chips consisted of a combination of canned meat and dry cereal. They practiced commands for long grueling hours, taking only short breaks for water. After dinner, which consisted of more canned meat and cereal, Chips accompanied Rowell to the *canteen* where he would doze while his partner watched *newsreels* and movies, or talked and played card games with the other soldiers. At nightfall, they stood together at attention while the bugler played *taps* and the flag was lowered, carefully folded, and put away until the next morning.

Chips had always been proud of the few tricks he had learned at home. Father had taught him to walk nicely on a leash. He could usually stop and sniff as much as he liked, and he was permitted to walk ahead of his companion as long as he didn't drag them down the street. Gail and Nan had taught him to raise his paw to shake whenever he performed a *sit.* When a ball or stick was thrown he was expected to fetch it back, and no one ever scolded him for barking when he heard a stranger's footsteps coming up the front walk. In fact, Mother often made a point of saying that he was a *good watchdog*. Chips quickly discovered the Army's rules were very different.

Chips learned to *sit, stay,* and *come* by following Rowell's silent hand signals. He learned to walk precisely at his left side whenever he was given the command to *heel,* and to never pull on his leash or wander aimlessly to the left or the right. He learned to crawl under barbed wire, creep through long dark tunnels, ford streams, and walk on shaky narrow boards placed twelve feet off the ground. When funny little balls called *hand grenades* were thrown he was never, under any circumstance, to fetch them back. When they went for overnight hikes, something the Army called *bivouacking,* and it was Chips's turn to *patrol,* he was not allowed to bark when he heard unfamiliar noises. Instead, Rowell praised him for *alerting* silently by standing perfectly still and bristling his *hackles.*

Chips also learned to play *war games,* and despite his first accidental encounter with a gas mask, he quickly learned to scrape along the ground on his belly with the contraption fixed over his head, while deafening guns blasted and shells exploded around him. Each day Chips practiced jumping over fences or leaping onto the backs of trucks. The higher he jumped the happier it seemed to make his new master, Rowell. *What would Mother say?* Chips sometimes thought.

Although Chips missed his home and family, his life with Private Rowell was full of new adventures. Chips enjoyed learning, and his young soldier was always patient and encouraging. By the end of six weeks Chips had learned many new tricks to take home to show Mother, Father, and the children.

"Chips, today you'll begin your serious training as a *sentry dog*," Rowell said proudly one morning. "Sergeant Hart agrees that you're not only smart enough for the job, but you're big enough to be a powerful attacker if the situation requires it."

Chips wagged his tail.

Unfortunately, the eager dog quickly discovered the *trick* Rowell wanted him to learn was both difficult and confusing. Not only had Mother trained him never to jump on people, but she had also taught him *NEVER* to bite. Chips's unfortunate accident with Charlie Wilson had so humiliated him that even the thought of a playful nip left him feeling queasy. Yet Rowell, the man who fed, groomed, worked, and played with him, the human Chips had grown to trust and respect during his weeks in the Army, was commanding him to attack and bite a complete stranger. It was more than Chips could bear.

To learn this new trick, Rowell instructed Chips to sit quietly at his side while a soldier Chips had never seen before slipped up behind them. As soon as the stranger drew close Rowell would say, *watch him*, and Chips was expected to jump up and grab the man's right arm, the arm usually used to carry a weapon. He had to hold his grasp until Rowell gave the command to *release*. But no matter how much Chips wanted to please and obey Rowell, he could not bring himself to *attack*, even when the soldier wore protective clothing.

"It's no use," Rowell complained to Sergeant Hart

one afternoon while they watched Chips diligently run through an obstacle course that had been set up for the dogs. "Chips moves faster and leaps higher than any other K-9 on the post. He alerts silently to danger. He understands every command I give him, but he refuses to attack. I think Chips is simply too kind to hurt a human."

"Give him a few more days," Hart responded. "When I met his family I could see he was a much beloved pet. It can take dogs from homes like these a little longer to adjust to our Army training."

"And what if he won't *attack*?"

"You know the answer to that, Private. We can't have a K-9 in a *battle theater* if they won't obey commands. We'll have to leave Chips behind."

Disheartened and discouraged, Rowell shook his head and called for Chips to *come*.

Chips obediently went to Rowell's side, wagging his tail happily in greeting.

"One more thing, Rowell," Sergeant Hart added. "When I was going through Chips's papers I noticed he hasn't been tattooed. Captain Hill usually doesn't forget something like that. Better get Chips over to the infirmary as soon as possible. All the K-9's need *brand numbers* before we ship out.

The next morning, instead of reporting to the training field, Rowell took Chips back to the infirmary. Chips eagerly looked for Captain Hill but he was nowhere to be found. Instead, a doctor he had never seen before met them at the door.

"I don't know how this K-9 has gone this long without getting a brand number," the doctor said in a cold and unfriendly tone. "It's against Army regulations."

"We've been so busy training it slipped my mind, sir," Rowell apologized.

"Well, hurry up and get him on the examining table, Private. The iron is hot and ready."

Rowell motioned for Chips to jump up, which he did easily and gracefully. He then instructed him to lie down and stay still.

Chips obeyed, but when he looked up and saw the steel-faced doctor coming toward him with a long stick in his hand he grew suspicious. His nose twitched from the intense heat at the end of the glowing red branding iron. Chips coiled back his muscles.

"Make certain he stays perfectly still," the doctor warned.

Before Chips could react, the doctor grabbed hold of his left ear. He heard a terrible hissing sound and felt a painful burning sensation fill his entire head. It was followed by the unpleasant odor of singed fur and flesh. Rage took control of every nerve ending in the giant dog's body. Chips lunged from the table and sank his fangs into the doctor's right arm.

The doctor screamed out in surprise and pain, which only made Chips hang on harder.

"*Release*!" Rowell shouted. "*Release*!"

Chips was in a daze but his handler's words registered and he slowly let go of his deadly grip.

"You did it, Chips," the young soldier exclaimed. "You attacked!"

"This is preposterous!" the doctor shouted as he

examined the bites on his arm. Fortunately, his several layers of clothing had protected him from the full impact of Chips's razor-sharp teeth.

"Gee, I'm really sorry, Captain. I hope you're not badly hurt, but Chips has never attacked anyone before, and I've been trying to teach him to attack for weeks. This is the best thing that's happened to me since I *enlisted* in the Army!"

"Have you gone raving mad, Private? This animal could have gravely injured me and you're applauding it? I'll have you *court-martialed* for this, and I'll have that mongrel shot!"

"What's all this?" Captain Hill asked as he stepped through the door in the nick of time. Fortunately, he was able to talk the angry doctor out of punishing Private Rowell, as well as convincing him to spare Chips's life. Although this last effort required a call from the colonel who guaranteed that Chips would soon be sent far away where he would never be able to harm the doctor again.

★ ★ ★

The following week, when Rowell went to get Chips, now officially K-9 Brand 11A, from his dog house, he proudly carried a new brown leather collar in his hand. "You've earned your working collar, old boy," he said. "From now on you'll wear it when we're on duty."

Chips sniffed the polished leather and barked his approval.

"Today begins the biggest adventure of our lives,"

Rowell continued. "Our platoon has been given orders to join the *Third Infantry Division* under *General George Patton's* command. We're going to sail from Newport News, Virginia all the way to Morocco. That's a country in North Africa! They need us to fight the French *Vichy* and capture the city of *Casablanca.* The Vichy have sided with the *Nazis,* so we're going to teach them a lesson they'll never forget."

The following week, when they boarded the train for Newport News, Chips joyfully wagged his tail. He felt certain he was finally going home to his family.

CHAPTER 9

ALL PAWS ON DECK

T he shipyard in Newport News was one of the busiest along the eastern seaboard. A massive fleet was preparing for the voyage to North Africa. The docks were lined with every kind of ship in the United States Navy. There were battleships, aircraft carriers, destroyers, cruisers, frigates, small gunboats, minesweepers, oil tankers, and troop transport ships. These vessels carried everything the soldiers and sailors would need for their two week journey across the Atlantic and the days of fighting ahead: ammunition, food, clothing, medical supplies, trucks, tanks, and airplanes. Some of the boats were like floating hotels and carried hundreds, even thousands, of men and women.

It was a dangerous passage. To avoid enemy submarines or U-boats that sometimes traveled in wolf packs the fleet was forced to zigzag its way across the ocean. In the end, 60,000 soldiers, the largest combat force that had ever been shipped from the United States, *sailed into battle. The secret military code name for the invasion was Operation Torch.*

★ ★ ★

Rowell and Chips slowly made their way through the crowded docks. Soldiers and sailors milled along the wharf talking, laughing, and putting their gear in order. Some carried large *duffle bags* over their shoulders or sat on *footlockers* that were filled with clothing and the few personal possessions they could take on the trip, including photographs and letters from loved ones at home. Others carried official-looking notepads and checklists and were helping to direct the men, women, and *cargo* onto the many ships.

"Take a look at that beauty, Chips!" Rowell exclaimed pointing to a powerful battleship that was anchored along the docks. "It's the USS Massachusetts. I bet she's at least five city blocks long. The Tuscaloosa and the Wichita are here too. They're two of our best battle cruisers. And out in the bay is the aircraft carrier Ranger. Look, you can see bomber planes lined up on the *flight deck.*"

Although Chips couldn't understand his partner's words his eyes sparkled and the tip of his tail wagged with shared enthusiasm.

As Rowell stood admiring the ships in the harbor Chips's attention was unexpectedly diverted by two soldiers who came sauntering toward them. For a moment, Chips could barely believe his eyes, ears, and nose. He immediately recognized Mr. Green and Charlie Wilson, dressed in their army *fatigues.* Completely forgetting his strict training, Chips broke free from his unsuspecting companion and raced at a gallop to greet his hometown friends. His entire body wriggled with excitement.

"Well I'll be... It's our Mr. Chips!" Mr. Green said. "Why you old devil. You really did join the Army." At this Chips jumped up and licked his friend's face from top to bottom and again from bottom to top.

Charlie Wilson retreated a few steps then bravely stepped forward as Chips turned to greet him. Understanding the old fear, Chips gently nuzzled the young soldier's palm then sat down and offered Charlie his paw to shake.

Meanwhile, Rowell was flustered and confused by Chips's sudden lack of discipline. "Heel!" he commanded as caught up to the little reunion. "I'm sorry, soldiers, but this is a war dog and petting isn't allowed. No one is allowed to handle him but...."

"Our apologies for not following the rules," Mr. Green answered with a wide grin. "We're Chips's pals from back home," he said as he explained to a confused Rowell how he and Charlie Wilson knew Chips.

"I'm happy to have met two of Chips's close friends," Rowell said when it was time for them to say their good-byes.

"He's a special one," Mr. Green said proudly. "Stay safe, old boy," he cautioned, giving the big dog a final pat on the head.

"So long, Mr. Chips," Charlie added. "Remember, we're going to give the enemy a whopping they won't forget. I'll be seeing you back home before you know it."

Chips sadly whimpered as his friends walked away and melted into the sea of soldiers and sailors.

Chips and Rowell then continued to weave their way through the crowded docks until they came to a long row of wooden crates. Each box had a small, screen-covered window, and Chips could make out the silhouettes of noses and ears inside many of them. Stenciled in bold letters on each box was written *U.S. ARMY DOG.*

"I'll take that paperwork," a big, burly-looking soldier said as he reached for the set of forms Rowell held up to him. After carefully scrutinizing the information he took a marker out of his pocket and wrote *Brand 11A* in thick black letters across the door of one of the boxes. "Place your dog in the crate, Private."

"Well, Chips, this is where we have to part, but I'll see you again when we get on board the boat." Rowell opened the door to the crate and gently nudged Chips in and secured the lock.

Chips peeked through the one small window and sadly watched his partner disappear from sight. Forlorn, he let out a few sharp barks in the hope that Rowell would return. Other crated dogs answered his bark and he was certain he heard Pal and Mena among them. Eventually Chips decided there was nothing left to do but lie down and wait. He put his soft muzzle between his front paws and fell into a fitful sleep.

Chips dreamed he was at home in his cozy spot next the fireplace. Mother was sewing as she usually did in the evenings, and Father was reading the newspaper. There was a knock at the front door. Chips ran to investigate but when he got to the entranceway the door swung open and he tumbled out into an empty sky. The yard, grass, and trees had all disappeared, and he was falling through space. Terrified, Chips awoke with a start.

His heart beat even faster when he realized he really *was* swinging through the air! A large crane was hoisting the bed of crates from the loading dock to the deck of the ship. When he looked out the window, Chips could see nothing but blue sky dissolving into azure water. Suddenly he felt his box descend, and then it jolted to a stop. He heard the sound of human voices, and after much maneuvering the door to his crate was opened.*

"Welcome aboard, Chips," Rowell said, greeting him.

At the sight of his partner Chips leapt up to give him a big wet kiss across his face, which in turn sent the surprised soldier sprawling onto his backside.

"Well, well, if it isn't my old friend K-9 Chips," a gruff voice spoke above the muffled laughter of the soldiers and sailors who had gathered around to greet the dogs. "And I suppose this an example of the *impeccable training* I can expect from you and your dog, Private?"

Chips did not need to see the colorful bars and glistening pins on the man's jacket to recognize his old acquaintance, the colonel.

---

* Later, dogs were walked onto the ships to avoid injury.

"Yes, sir, I mean no, Colonel," Rowell stuttered as he stood and brushed himself off.

"Let's see whether or not K-9 Chips can follow the rules for once. I'll be keeping my eyes on both of you."

"Yes, sir,"

The colonel turned toward Sergeant Hart. "All dogs must be crated for the night by *2100 hours*. No dogs are allowed on the Captain's *bridge* or below deck unless it's for *sickbay* or severe weather. We sail tomorrow at dawn."

"Yes, sir," Hart replied.

"As colonel, my duties are to the entire *brigade*. I don't have time for the shenanigans of one K-9 platoon. Why I ever promised headquarters I would oversee this war dog program I'll never know. I should have my head examined. But as long as I'm responsible for its success, I want to hear about any K-9 that steps out of line. Is that clear?"

"Perfectly clear, sir,"

"And one last thing."

"Yes, sir?"

"These waters are infested with wolf packs. See that the men and dogs are prepared."

Both soldiers and K-9's watched as the colonel removed his gold watch from his waist pocket and noted the time. Then he put it away and headed for the bridge.

"Okay men," Sergeant Hart said. "You heard the old man's warning. He's right—the waters will be full of enemy U-boats. Give the dogs some fresh air and then we'll meet back here at 1100 hours to review the *battle stations drill.*"

"I guess you're about to become a sea dog, Chips," Rowell said. "We may as well get started with our ship routine now." He put the leather collar on Chips's neck and they jogged around the deck for their daily exercise.

Much to Chips's delight both Pal and Mena were on board too. That evening all three wagged tails, sniffed, and touched noses in the traditional friendly greeting. Pal, as always, was full of energy, but Mena was not quite herself. Chips sensed there was something different about her. Mena's doe-like eyes looked weary, and rather than romp and play she preferred to go to her crate and sleep.

★   ★   ★

The next morning Chips was awakened by the sound of the bugler. As he peered through the small screen window of his crate he could distinguish human forms busily moving around the deck. He sensed excitement and anticipation in their quick steps.

"Out you go, old boy," Rowell smiled as he opened the crate door. "It's a grand day for sailing."

No sooner had Chips taken a deep breath of the crisp autumn air than a sharp whistle blew and their ship heaved away from port. Nearby on the docks a band played *Anchors Away,* and he heard the sound of cheering voices.

All the soldiers and sailors, including Rowell, rushed to lean over the side rails and wave to the crowd of well-wishers who had risen early to see them off. People waved flags and threw colorful confetti into the air.

Rowell motioned for Chips to put his front paws on the ship's railing to view the fanfare. Chips was surprised to see families with small children lining the docks. Excitedly, he scanned the crowd and sniffed the air, hoping to detect his own family. He felt certain that with so many children Gail, Nan, and John must be among them.

Yet instead of the families being united with loved ones, the boat began to move out into the water, and the people on shore began to shrink as they drifted further and further away. Chips was so dismayed he raised his head to the sky and let out a long and mournful husky's howl. This only caused the crowds on the wharf to shout and wave with even greater enthusiasm. Rowell, understanding Chips's confusion, pulled him away from the rail and knelt down to comfort him.

"I know it's hard for you to understand, Chips, because you're only a dog, but we have an important job to do. We have to do our share to end this war. Then we can go *home*."

Something in what Rowell said sounded familiar and reassuring. Then Chips remembered. These were the sounds of Mother's words. Chips knew Rowell, like Mother, cared about him, and that he wouldn't ask him to do something he didn't think was right and good. Chips nuzzled Rowell's shoulder with his nose to let him know he trusted him.

"I have a special surprise for you," Rowell continued. "It arrived when we were still in Front Royal. I was saving it for when we were at sea, but I think you should have it now. Stay here and I'll be back." As Rowell spoke he gave Chips the hand signal to lie down and wait for him to return.

Chips obediently did as he was told. A few minutes later Rowell came back with a brown paper package in his hand. It was addressed to: *K-9 CHIPS, FRONT ROYAL WAR DOG CENTER* in a child's handwriting. Chips did not need to have the package unwrapped to know its contents. He could smell the delicious aroma of homemade peanut butter cookies through the wrapping.

"These are the best cookies I've ever tasted," Rowell said as he fed Chips two of the carefully packed treats and munched on one himself.

Chips could not have agreed more. Once he was satiated he lay down to rest and enjoy the sunny morning on the ship's deck.

At first Chips didn't feel anything unusual. The gentle rocking of the vessel as it cut through Chesapeake Bay was nearly undetectable, but the moment they reached the open ocean a terrible feeling came over him. It was an awful, queasy feeling in his stomach, like the time he had eaten Gail's entire strawberry cream-filled birthday cake, including the candles, while the children played pin-the-tail-on-the-donkey in the next room.

"What's up, old boy?" Rowell asked when Chips rolled over on his side and moaned. "You don't look too good." No matter how hard he tried, the young soldier couldn't get the sorrowful-looking dog back on his legs.

"I'd say your partner's seasick," Sergeant Hart observed when he saw Chips. "Mena looks a bit *green around the edges* too. And so do some of the men, for that matter."

All along the ship's rails soldiers were standing with their heads hung the over the sides, feeling much the way Chips did.

"Don't worry, you'll get used to it," a seasoned sailor said who stopped by to help. "Sickbay is handing out sea-sickness pills for both men and K-9's."

The pills helped Chips and many of the men, but not Mena. No amount of seasickness pills could make her act like her chipper old self. She had no interest in running, playing, or even eating. Her handler finally gave up and allowed her to stay in her crate for the better part of each day.

★ ★ ★

Once his seasickness passed, Chips thought life aboard ship was more fun than boot camp. The dogs' crates were placed in a single row on each side of the deck facing out toward the sunlight and water. Chips's crate was between Pal's and Mena's. Although Mena spent most of her days sleeping, it was a comfort to know she was nearby.

After jogging around the deck each morning the dogs ate their usual breakfast and rested while the soldiers cleaned the ship. When they finished, the colonel would tour the boat with the ship's captain, who always wore a starched white suit with flashy gold buttons. If either officer discovered the smallest fragment of dirt or litter the men would be called upon to clean the entire ship again. The colonel would then lecture his soldiers about the importance of cleanliness on the ship. He always ended his speech by reminding everyone that dogs were not allowed below deck or on the bridge, the place from which the ship's captain commandeered the vessel.

Once the men passed their daily inspection they had plenty of free time to play with the dogs. They devised all kinds of games and tricks to teach the K-9's new skills. Chips's favorite was called *search*. The soldiers would hide objects and the dogs would take turns searching for them. They hid everything from socks and toothbrushes to small rings and coins. Chips and Pal were the best at this game, and the soldiers often argued about who had the better K-9.

"I have a proposal to make," Pal's handler, who was called Cobbs, announced to Rowell one afternoon after a fight broke out over whether Chips or Pal had been the first to find a hidden comb.

"What's that?"

"I say we have a search contest between Chips and Pal. The dog that wins will be declared the ship's champion."

"Fine. I'll not only accept the challenge but I'll wager you two weeks pay on Chips," Rowell said proudly.

"You're on. Two week's pay it is."

Some of the other soldiers and sailors standing nearby wagered their paychecks too. By the next day nearly everyone, except for the captain and the colonel who were unaware of the contest, had made a comparable bet.

The only thing the men had trouble deciding about

was what to hide. Rowell suggested one of Sergeant Hart's whistles, but it was agreed that the dogs knew the object all too well. A young sailor, who didn't know much about dogs, suggested hiding one of the cook's hats but the others quickly convinced him the cooking odors would make the search too easy.

Then Cobbs had an idea. "What about the colonel's pocket watch? I hear he hangs it on the back of his door every night before he goes to bed."

"But how will we get it if it's in his private quarters?" Rowell asked.

"His assistant owes me a favor for a little bet I helped him win awhile back. I'll see if he can slip the watch out of the colonel's room after he falls asleep. We'll only be borrowing it for short time. He'll never even know it's gone."

"Sounds a bit risky, but...."

"Fine," Cobbs said, not waiting to hear more. "I'll arrange for look-outs just in case the big brass decide to take a midnight stroll on deck."

★   ★   ★

The soldiers talked about the contest for days. Naturally, Rowell and Cobbs trained their dogs for the competition at every opportunity.

"Listen, Chips," Rowell said in his most serious tone of voice. "When I give the order to search, don't pay a bit of attention to Pal. Your nose is a hundred times better than his, and I'd wager a full month's pay on that fact."

Chips proudly wagged his tail at his friend's praise and picked up a rubber ball to play fetch, but Rowell ignored him and instead showed him a pocketknife he planned to hide for practice. After days of playing *search,* however, Chips had grown weary of the game. He often missed his afternoons playing 'fetch' in the grassy yard with the children and now, on the ship, he missed them even more. Yet to please Rowell he half-heartedly looked for the hidden pocketknife.

They were only two days away from their destination of North Africa when the men decided to hold the contest. As planned, after midnight, the lookouts were posted. One of the sailors showed Pal and Chips the colonel's gold timepiece. Each dog examined it carefully. Then the dogs were placed in their crates while the watch was hidden near the *stern* of the ship, inside a barrel of old ropes. When the time was right, Rowell and Cobbs let Pal and Chips out of their crates. Below deck, the men eagerly waited for the contest's results.

"Go search!" both handlers commanded.

Pal immediately took off for the stern of the boat.

"Go find the colonel's watch," Rowell urged Chips.

Chips looked up at Rowell and yawned.

As far as Chips was concerned, it was one thing to play this game in the middle of the day, but to play it in the middle of the night was asking too much. He didn't see that it should matter to Rowell if he was not in the mood, so he flopped down on the deck and yawned again.

"How dare you disobey my command!" Rowell scolded.

Never, in all their weeks of training together, had Rowell ever spoken in anger at him. Chips flinched as the harsh words stung his feelings.

"Go search!" Rowell growled.

Chips pulled himself up, and with his head dejectedly down sulkily walked toward the *bow* of the ship, the opposite direction Pal had taken.

Chips felt sad and confused. He knew that to disobey Rowell's command was a very bad thing, but he didn't understand why what had been only a game was suddenly so important to his friend and partner.

Rowell, infuriated at Chips's disobedience, threw up his arms in disgust and walked away.

As Chips plodded along the side of the deck brooding over his rough treatment, something far out in the water caught his eye. It was a small red light that flickered so briefly he wasn't certain he had really seen anything at all. He paused, staring out through the ship's railing, to see if it would return. The light blinked again in the blackened night. Chips decided to get a better look so he quickly climbed up several sets of steep stairs to gain the advantage of a higher viewing point. When he reached the uppermost deck of the forbidden Captain's bridge he spotted the mysterious light again. Having grown up as a vigilant watchdog, Chips had learned from the time he was a puppy to bark at anything suspicious in his surroundings. In an instant, he completely forgot his Army training to alert silently. Instead, Chips began wildly howling and barking at the threatening presence in the inky black water.

"What's that dog doing on the bridge!" shouted the

young officer who had left his post to join Rowell, Cobbs, and the other men for the *search* contest.

Rowell heard his partner's barks and immediately ran to find him. He bounded up the steps three at a time. "Chips, you know you're not allowed up here," he scolded.

Yet there was something sinister about the light Chips didn't like and no one, not even Rowell, could silence him.

"What the devil is all this racket about? I'll have that animal shot!" shouted the colonel who had been awakened by the barking from a sound sleep. He stopped abruptly when he recognized Chips. His face flushed and his eyes looked as though they could shoot sparks. Just as he was about to erupt like a volcano Rowell pointed out to the horizon.

"There," he said. "A red light. It could be a *periscope* on an enemy sub."

The colonel saw it too. He shouted a warning to the bridge, "*Sound general quarters!*"

"Sound general quarters!" echoed the ship's captain who had also been jolted awake by the barking. "U-boat off the *starboard bow*. All men on deck!"

"Rowell, tell Hart to have the men remove the dogs from their crates and report to their assigned battle stations," the colonel called over his shoulder as he ran to take his position near the ship's captain.

"Right away, Colonel."

When they returned to the crates most of the men had already gathered to retrieve their dogs. Pal stood proudly with the colonel's gold pocket watch in his mouth, but with the threat of the enemy vessel no one thought about the contest or the winner. Sergeant Hart took roll call. Everyone was accounted for except Mena and her partner. They were nowhere to be found.

"Has anyone seen Mena?" Hart asked.

"The last time Chips and I saw them was at dinner," Rowell answered.

"We don't have time to look for them now. The colonel said to man all battle stations."

"But we're just a troop ship," Cobbs said, looking worried. "We don't have the capability to fight a sub."

No sooner had Cobbs spoken than a light flashed in the distance. An American heavy cruiser was firing at the U-boat.

"There'll be fish in the water now," said one of the soldiers referring to the enemy's *torpedoes.* "They're sure to retaliate."

"Come on, Chips," Rowell said motioning for him to follow. "We'd better make ourselves useful."

They quickly stationed themselves near a cluster of guns, but while Rowell busied himself with helping one of the ship's gunners, Chips slipped away unnoticed.

Being of both collie and shepherd blood meant Chips was a herder by nature. At home, he had always kept an accounting of his family, making mental notes of the comings and goings of Mother, Father, and the children. He was particularly watchful with John, who often toddled off in an unpredictable fashion. Now, on the darkened deck of the ship, Chips fretted over the whereabouts of Mena and her handler.

After taking several moments to sniff the air for

Mena's scent and having no luck, Chips went back to her crate to begin his search. He located her trail and *tracked* it to the stairs that led below deck. Since all the soldiers and sailors were at their stations there was no one to prevent him from going below. Chips quickly made his way down the steep ladder staircase. He was winding his way through the maze of corridors when something jolted the ship and sent him and everything around him flying.

For a few moments Chips lay stunned in the middle of the dimly lit hallway. An enemy torpedo had grazed the side of their vessel and he had been knocked headfirst into a wall. He struggled to regain his senses. His head throbbed from the blow and he blinked away blood from a gash over his right eye. Chips steadied himself on his now wobbly legs and made his way down two more sets of stairs.

The ceilings were low and crossed with pipes and ventilation ducts. There were eerie moaning and creaking sounds coming from the various nooks and crannies. Chips barked to see if Mena would answer, but all he could hear was his own bark echoed back to him. He advanced a few paces and announced himself again but this time his call was returned with a strange sort of squeaking noise. The sound came from one of the storage rooms used for linens. Chips went to investigate.

Chips cautiously entered the small room. Curled up on a pile of blankets in a dark corner was a frightened but proud Mena surrounded by six squirming puppies. She was too weak to bark but she managed to wag her tail once or twice at the sight of Chips. Next to Mena, lying face down on the ground, was her handler. Chips knew something was wrong. He saw a small spot of blood on the soldier's temple and sniffed him cautiously. The man was still alive but the sensitive dog knew he needed help. Chips immediately went to get Rowell.

On deck the soldiers and crew had witnessed a full fire interchange between the American battleship and the submarine. The battleship had come within feet of being hit but had managed to evade the enemy and sent the U-boat running for safe water. Luckily their own troop ship had been saved. Chips found Rowell standing with the other dogs and handlers and barked to get his attention.

"Take it easy, boy," Rowell said. "The enemy's gone. They won't bother us again. The captain says we were grazed but we'll have that patched up tonight," Then he noticed the gash over Chips's eye. "What's this? You're bleeding!"

Chips backed away from Rowell in the direction of the stairs.

"Where are you going, Chips? I can't help you if you run away from me."

Chips barked excitedly. He continued to stay an arm's length out of reach as he lured Rowell toward the stairs that led below deck.

When they reached the opening Rowell shook his head. "Sorry, I can't let you go down there. It's against regulations. You know K-9's aren't allowed below deck."

Ignoring him, Chips turned and bounded down the steep stairs.

"Hey, wait. Come back. That's an order!" Rowell shouted as he nearly fell head over heels trying to catch him. "Maybe the colonel's right about you. You'll never be able to follow the rules!"

The young soldier chased Chips down two more flights of stairs and into the linen room. When Rowell saw Mena and her handler he understood why Chips had misbehaved the way he did. He quickly ran back for help.

★　★　★

"I've got to admit you had me pretty angry," Rowell said the next morning as he put a clean dressing on the cut over Chips's eye. "But if it hadn't been for you we might not have spotted the enemy's periscope in time, and Mena's handler's condition could have grown a lot worse. He must have been knocked unconscious when the torpedo hit us. Contest or not, to my mind, you're the best search dog on this ship."

Mena, who had been listening to their conversation from a makeshift *whelping box* the men had built for her and the puppies, barked her appreciation.

Suddenly a voice came over the ship's loudspeaker: *Soldiers should check their combat gear. All howitzers going ashore are to be inspected and broken down for transport. Embarkation begins tomorrow at 0500 hours.*

At that moment the colonel strode up to the men and dogs. "Chips, Pal, Scout, and Watch will go with the first *assault*. The rest of the K-9's will wait for further orders."

"Did you hear that, Chips?" Rowell said. "We're in the first group to go into battle!" Pal, Scout, and Watch's partner exchanged *high-fives* and the dogs enthusiastically jumped and pranced around them.

Mena whimpered as she watched her friends' excitement at the news. She wanted to join them, but she also knew that her first duty was to stay on the ship and care for her puppies.

"And one more thing, Private Rowell," the colonel continued. "See that Chips follows orders and stays low and quiet in the landing craft, if that's not too much to ask. I've told Hart to keep special tabs on you two."

"No, sir. I mean yes, sir."

"There'll be big sea swells out there tomorrow, and it's easy enough to swamp these *Higgins boats* in calm water without some crazy mutt going loco."

"Yes, sir."

"Another thing,"

"Yes, Colonel,"

"If you and Cobbs make it through this invasion you'll be in charge of polishing my pocket watch every day until you're either discharged from the Army or, if I get lucky, transferred to someone else's command.

"Yes, sir."

"Other colonels in this Army need only concern themselves with their brigades. I have to baby-sit a war dog platoon!" The colonel muttered to himself as he walked away.

That night after dinner the soldiers were especially quiet. Some of them sat along the edge of the deck writing letters home to their families and friends. Others read the bible or favorite poems. Chips, feeling Rowell's melancholy mood, leaned against his knee while his friend composed a letter to his parents.

"Dear Mom and Dad," he read aloud. "I have exciting news. I'm on a ship off the coast of Morocco. In case you don't know, that's in North Africa. Our invasion begins tomorrow before dawn. We're going to fight the French Vichy and take back the city of Casablanca. The Vichy government is under control of the Nazis. Someday we're going to liberate all of France and make it free again. I want you to know I'm not scared or worried about tomorrow's invasion one bit because Chips will be by my side and he's the best war dog in the whole United States Army."

With these words, Chips sat up at attention and proudly thumped his tail on the ship's wooden deck.

CHAPTER 10

OPERATION TORCH

O n November 8th 1942, nearly one year after the Japanese attacked Pearl Harbor, American forces landed in North Africa with the goal of capturing the key city of Casablanca. It was the first major invasion of American forces during World War II. The military's goal was to drive the Vichy govern- ment, which was under the control of the Nazis, out of the region. This would help them to gain a foothold from which they could attack Rommel, the leader of the Nazi army in North Africa. The Battle of Casablanca, also known as Operation Torch, was a strategically important one for the Allied forces.

★   ★   ★

"Stay down and keep quiet," Rowell calmly directed Chips as they boarded the landing boat.

There was a sharp chill in the air, and Chips shuddered as he climbed down into the small craft. He could see nothing but murky seawater surrounding him. The thought of water, especially a lot of it, still terrified him, but he dutifully obeyed his partner's command. They had to move quickly because enemy submarines had been spotted and general quarters had been sounded. Pal was sitting in front of Chips, and Scout and Watch were following in another boat.

"It's so dark I can't make out the shoreline," Cobbs whispered to Rowell. "Did you hear the sailors talking about the coral reefs? They say they're sharp enough to tear the bottom out of a boat four times the size of this bathtub. If that happens to us, we'll drown for sure with these sixty pound packs on our backs."

Worried, Rowell looked at Chips. The dogs also wore vests strapped to their bodies. The vests had deep pockets that were weighted down with tools, medical aids, and other supplies. But Rowell's thoughts were interrupted as a large wave of seawater washed over the side of the boat, soaking the men, dogs, and gear.

"Hold your packs over your heads when we hit the next swell," directed Sergeant Hart who was sitting next to Rowell. "The salt water might jam the guns."

Chips shivered with cold and fear as the seawater sprayed over them. Yet when he looked up and saw the frightened look in Rowell's eyes, he forgot his own dread of the water and reassuringly pushed his muzzle into his partner's gloved hand.

"You're a good pal, Chips. We'll watch out for each other and we'll make it through this crazy war," Rowell placed his hand on the big dog's head as he spoke.

Cobbs turned around and whispered to Rowell. "Why is it so quiet along the beach? It's too quiet, if you ask me." At that moment the white beam of a searchlight pierced the air from the shore.

"They've spotted us now," Rowell answered.

"I can't tell who's shivering more, Pal or me."

Rowell pointed into the sky. "A *tracer* from one of our ships." A red light tracked across the sky and exploded near the source of the white beam, somewhere in the blackened hillside. "That's it! The fighting's started!"

At the sound of the first explosions Chips barely flinched, but as the pounding shells intensified his body began to tremble. An enemy battery on shore fired at their landing boat. Chips could hear bullets hitting the water around them. When he tried to peer over the side Rowell pulled him back.

"Stay down," Rowell sharply commanded. Chips flattened his body onto the bottom of the boat as his partner protectively leaned over him. Chips could hear the young soldier's heart pounding through the thick layers of combat clothing. Overhead, enemy torpedo planes swooped down on the vessels, strafing them with bullets as they tried to land close to the beaches. One boat, caught up on a reef was a sitting duck. Its men jumped overboard only moments before an enemy bomber dropped a bulls-eye on their craft, making it explode in a flash of red sparks and flames.

Suddenly Chips's boat jolted to a stop as it grounded on a sandbar. An enemy plane flew low overhead and dropped a bomb dangerously close. The explosion shook the boat and deafened the men and dogs' hearing. Another fighter plane showered the shoreline with bullets. Billowing clouds of black smoke blinded everyone on board.

"Everybody out!" Sergeant Hart commanded.

The men didn't wait to de-board in orderly fashion. Instead, they charged off the lowered front ramp into the dark water and struggled toward shore.

Chips leapt off too, sputtering and gagging on the salt-water. It was up to his neck, and he half walked, half paddled, next to Rowell's booted leg. The water was deep in parts, and the vest with its pockets of supplies weighted him down. Rowell had to scoop his arm under Chip's belly to keep him from sinking in the turbulent surf.

By the time the two reached the beach they were forced to climb over wounded soldiers, some of them their friends.

"Keep moving!" Hart shouted as he bravely directed his men to safety.

Chips and Rowell ran zigzag along the beach to avoid being hit by bullets. A hand grenade exploded close to them. Flying gravel and sand stung their faces and eyes but they kept moving. They didn't stop running until they reached a clump of high grass and dunes beyond the field of gunfire.

Rowell shouted something to Chips as he searched his pack, but the sounds of exploding shells drowned out his words.

Large gasoline fires from downed planes and hit vehicles burned along the beach. Enemy torpedo planes and bombers continued to target the landing boats. Two heavy cruisers, the Tuscaloosa and the Wichita pounded out rounds from their cannons. High over the water three *American Wildcats* successfully shot three enemy fighters out of the sky. In the far distance, the USS Massachusetts fired on the French battleship the Jean Bart, crippling it. The smoke-filled sky glowed red as the dawn sliced open the horizon.

"Paw!" Rowell shouted into Chips's ear. "Give me your paw!" He gently held the dog's leg in his hands and examined it. Blood was oozing from the pads.

Chips had been so frightened he hadn't felt the sharp shells and pieces of coral cutting him as he waded to shore.

Rowell carefully tended to his partner, tightly wrapping each leg in gauze. "That should keep the sand out."

Chips gave Rowell's hand an appreciative lick.

At that moment three American soldiers dove behind their patch of grass and sand dunes. It was nearly impossible to make out their features as their faces were blackened by soot and their uniforms caked with sand. When they brushed themselves off Rowell could see two of them were young officers with lieutenant's bars on their sleeves. The third man was older and wore a major's insignia on his uniform.

"What's that?" mouthed one of the lieutenants pointing at Chips.

"A wolf!" shouted his peer, but his words were lost in the barrage of explosions.

"Haven't you two idiots ever heard of a war dog?" bellowed the major.

Both men shook their heads *no*.

The major turned to Rowell and quickly explained his situation. "We got separated from our *company*. Our mission was to slip this colonel behind enemy lines to arrange a *cease-fire*. Our captain was hit, and I don't know what happened to the colonel. Now we have to go it alone." He pulled a map out of his jacket, and motioned to the others to gather around him. "The enemy *batteries* along this ridge have been put out of commission. If we follow along here," he drew an imaginary line with his finger, "we can try to make contact with a high-ranking officer to get us through to Vichy headquarters in Casablanca." The major pointed at Chips. "What's your K-9 trained for?"

"Chips is mostly trained for sentry work, but he's good at *scouting* and *patrolling* too," Rowell added proudly.

"He may come in handy if we...." but the major never got to finish his sentence. A shell whistled toward them and they all dove deeper into the dunes for cover. As soon as they had recovered from the blast the major waved for them to follow him.

As they crept farther behind the enemy lines and away from the fighting their surroundings grew almost quiet. Eventually, only the distant rumblings of gunfire and shells interrupted the otherwise peaceful morning. Chips was relieved they were moving away from the loud explosions, and he began to relax and enjoy the morning's hike with the soldiers. He even paused for a moment to watch a small rabbit scamper out of a bush and disappear over a nearby hill. He felt a twinge of homesickness for his favorite woods back home.

"Why's the dog stopping, Private?" one of the lieutenants asked.

"A rabbit," Rowell replied.

"What's the big deal about a rabbit?" The soldier turned to his friend. "Hey, Eddie, we got us a war dog that's afraid of bunny rabbits."

Both men snickered.

"He isn't alerting. He's just curious." Rowell had taken a quick disliking to both of the major's junior officers.

They walked for another half-mile when Chips stopped again. This time his body language was different. He stood frozen like a statue with his ears cocked forward, listening. Only the fur along the ridge of his back bristled.

Rowell knew Chips detected danger and he crouched low and readied his rifle. The major, also seeing Chips alert, did the same. But the two lieutenants, oblivious to both the K-9's warning and their superior officer's hand motions, continued to walk around a bend in the path, straight into a trap. They were immediately surrounded by Vichy soldiers who ordered them to drop their weapons to the ground. Both lieutenants turned to look back for the major and Rowell for help. This action only forewarned the enemy. Moments later, Rowell, the major, and Chips were surrounded too.

Having never seen or heard foreigners before, Chips growled and bared his teeth.

"*Un loup!*" exclaimed one of the soldiers in French, thinking Chips was a *wolf*. The others backed away in fear. Then one of them pointed his rifle at Chips's head.

"No, he's a dog. *Il est un chien!*" Rowell shouted in poorly spoken French, protectively stepping in front of Chips. Fortunately, one of the soldiers understood a little English and waved for his comrade to put away his gun.

"*Un chien? Mais, Il est très grand!*"

"Yes, he's a big dog all right," Rowell said and directed Chips to lie down so he would be less intimidating. The man who had pointed the gun still looked frightened enough to do something foolish. Chips was suspicious of the strange-sounding men and wanted to be on the ready, but he obeyed Rowell's order.

The Vichy soldiers spoke among themselves for several minutes, occasionally motioning toward the Americans and Chips. Eventually they seemed to be in agreement and signaled for the Americans to walk in the direction of their camp. After trekking several miles they arrived at a cluster of tents with many other soldiers. Everyone gathered around Rowell and Chips, asking questions in French that Rowell and the other three Americans couldn't understand or answer. The Vichy soldiers seemed convinced Chips was at least part wolf.

"*Bonjour,* gentlemen, what do we have here?" a distinguished looking French officer asked as he parted the crowd. When he saw the higher-ranking major he spoke directly to him in clear and concise English.

"Welcome to our humble camp, Major. Is there anything I may do to make your stay with us more comfortable?"

"I need to get a message to your commanding officers. We wish to offer conditions for a cease-fire. "

The French officer's eyebrows arched up. "Ah yes, my radio communications have indicated we are slowly losing ground to your troops. As they say in your Hollywood westerns, *you have us outnumbered*. I will see you are safely taken to our headquarters provided the dog and his soldier remain here. My men have grown bored with camp life and this *wolf-dog* makes them smile."

The major didn't know what to say. As Rowell's acting superior officer he was responsible for his welfare.

"Don't worry, Major. I'll be fine as long as I have Chips with me," Rowell reassured him. "You have an important mission to accomplish."

"Stay safe, Private," the major said and gave Chips a last goodbye stroke on the top of his head. Then he and the two lieutenants hastily departed with their Vichy escort.

One of the soldiers who spoke a little English asked if Chips could perform tricks. Rowell showed them how he could fetch and find hidden objects and obey hand signals. The men laughed and applauded each time Chips performed. Although Chips was weary from the long hike and his paws hurt from the cuts, he enjoyed the attention and cheers from the strange-sounding men.

After nearly an hour of performing, several soldiers arrived with baskets of food for lunch. They gathered in small groups and passed around wine, bread, cheese, and sausages. Both Rowell and Chips had completely forgotten about food until this moment. Now they couldn't believe their good fortune. The enemy soldiers generously offered them as much food as they wanted.

Rowell was careful not to drink the wine, but when the sausages were passed to him he looked at Chips and smiled. "I know Army regulations say K-9's aren't allowed sausages, but I think we can make an exception today. Besides, I can't think of a soldier who deserves them more," he added and fed Chips a big hunk of the delicious meat.

Afterward, Chips licked his partner's face to show his deep appreciation.

When lunch was finished the soldiers drifted off to shady spots to take afternoon naps. Rowell instructed Chips to lie next to him. In the far distance the faint rumblings of the bombardment could still be heard.

"We have to get back to our platoon, Chips," Rowell whispered. "We need to escape."

As soon as he was certain the other soldiers were fully asleep, Rowell motioned for Chips to crawl snake-like on his belly toward a thicket of trees. Chips followed his partner's instructions, and they slithered to safety.

When they were out of earshot Rowell gave Chips his order: "Go find Hart and the others; Take us home."

Home.

Chips had never been given a command like this before, but he knew what *home* meant, and he knew that where he had left his friends on the beach was the way back to his family—to Mother, Father, and the children. He immediately set off in the direction of the battle guns.

They had hiked through thick brambles and rocky

terrain for nearly an hour when they paused for a moment to catch their breath along the base of a steep incline. Rowell was about to share a drink of water from his *canteen* with Chips when a pleasantly familiar scent arrested the dog's keen senses. Chips stopped, lifted his head, and carefully sniffed the air. He detected the same delicious aroma of sausages the enemy soldiers had so generously shared at lunch. Chips's mouth watered at the thought of another taste of the spicy meat.

"What is it?" Rowell whispered and readied his rifle under his shoulder.

Although Chips wanted to go home more than anything else in the world, and he understood his immediate orders were to return to his platoon, he simply couldn't resist the possibility of getting one more bite of the delectable treat along the way. Chips scampered up the rocky slope. Trusting in his K-9's sense of direction, Rowell scrambled up the steep incline after him.

Chips traversed the top of the hill several times, but every time he thought he had located the source of the scent, it faded on the breeze.

"What's gotten into you?" Rowell asked as he watched his partner dart back and forth with his nose to the wind. "You can't have lost our path back. We're so close now. The guns are much louder."

Yet Chips continued his erratic pacing. He knew precisely how to get back to the men on the beach, but he also knew the sausages were close by: very close. Chips stealthily made his way down the hillside and up the next with Rowell in tow. When he reached the hill's crescent he stopped. Below them, poorly camouflaged in brush and leaves, was an enemy *artillery tank.*

Rowell quickly pulled Chips behind some rocks so they wouldn't be seen.

As they watched, a soldier poked his head out of the opening at the top of the tank and surveyed the landscape with binoculars he held raised in one hand. But it was what he held in his other hand that arrested Chips's attention. It was a lump of the delicious meat. The man took a bite, swung the binoculars around, and took another bite. Chips's tail wagged and he started forward.

Rowell quickly grabbed his collar and silently directed him to *stay.*

As soon as the enemy disappeared into the armored vehicle Rowell whispered in Chips's ear. "Are you trying to get us killed? I'm the one who gives the commands. If that tank gunner had seen us they would have blown us sky high, and half the hill along with us. We'll stay here until it gets dark, then we'll try to slip past them."

Chips sighed gloomily and rested his head on his front paws. Not only was the sausage off limits, but he had also made Rowell angry and placed them in harm's way. He had let his stomach distract him from his mission. *Home* seemed very far away. The hours passed in the bleak and isolated landscape. Eventually, the sun began to sink lower in the western sky.

The day had been an exhausting one, and Chips was about to drift into a light sleep when he detected the sound of more voices: American voices. He waited and listened as they gradually drew closer. Chips looked down at the enemy artillery tank and then in the direction of the approaching men. It didn't take long for the shrewd dog to realize the Americans were walking directly into danger. He knew he needed to warn them. His body went rigid and his hackles stood on end.

"Well, I'm glad to see you finally understand we've got an enemy tank sitting in front of us," Rowell whispered sarcastically. "It's about time you alerted."

Chips could hear the voices getting closer and he softly whined.

Rowell, whose hearing was only as good as any man's, detected nothing. "There're times when I worry the colonel's right about you. We've got rules for a reason...." but he stopped in the middle of his sentence.

Without warning, Chips leapt onto all four legs and dashed to the highest point on the hill. Then he put his head in the air and let out a mournful wolf-like howl. The howl came from the depths of his husky soul: it was a cry that had been passed from generation to generation through thousands of years, a call to his pack that warned of imminent danger.

"What's that sound, Corporal?" A young American private asked nervously.

"That's a wolf if I've ever hear one. And I've heard a lot of them back home in Wyoming."

"Do they have wolves in North Africa?"

"Beats me, Private," the corporal responded. "It could be a trap. Better stay down and be ready."

"Corporal, look!" The soldier's face stiffened with fear as he pointed to the rise on a nearby hill.

The rays of the setting sun illuminated and magnified the great dog's silhouette as he stood howling with all his might. Even more terrified than the Americans were the two Vichy soldiers inside the tank. They were already nervous and edgy about having to spend so many hours secluded in the barren terrain. Upon poking his head out of the hatch and seeing what he believed was a larger-than-life bloodthirsty fiend, the spooked gunner gave the order to abandon their position. In fact, the unsuspecting Americans were nearly run over by the fleeing tank.

"Your dog saved our lives," praised the corporal later when he met Rowell. "We would have walked right into a trap. I heard we had a war dog *detachment* with us but I never met one until now. Chips is one heck of a soldier."

★   ★   ★

Later that evening, when Chips was resting in the makeshift camp, he watched and listened as the soldiers conversed amongst themselves. They talked about their battle experiences and the certain victory ahead. Then, as always, their talk turned toward home. As Chips listened to them reminisce about the places and friends and families they had left behind, his dog's heart opened wide to them. His instinct, as old as his race, told him he must guard and protect these young soldiers until they could return to their loved ones, and he could go back to his own family. Chips finally understood he had an important job to do and he felt content. So content that he put his head on his front paws, and for the first time since joining the Army, fell into a deep and satisfying sleep.

CHAPTER 11

GUARDING THE PRESIDENT

"The United States Army works in mysterious ways," the colonel said as he paced back and forth in his tent. "It's not my job to question orders from my superiors but to obey them," he scowled as he spoke. "I've just received orders for several K-9's to work as sentry dogs for a very important meeting taking place here in Casablanca in three days. Sergeant Hart believes you and Chips are capable of handling this assignment."

The colonel looked at Rowell and Chips and sighed. "I'm personally giving you these orders, rather than Hart, because some *VERY* important people will be attending this conference and there's no room for mistakes on the part of soldiers or dogs. Do you understand me, Private?"

"Yes sir, Colonel. Chips and I are always prepared...."

"Prepared to break the rules!" interjected the

colonel, his face reddening. "Don't get me wrong, Private, I've always believed Chips has the potential to be a top war dog. Never would have brought him over here with Hart's unit if I didn't. But like I always say, the Army doesn't have room for K-9's who can't obey commands." With these words he brought his fist down hard on his *field desk.*

Chips, who liked the colonel despite his gruffness, cheerfully thumped his own tail on the floor.

"What's more, I'd like to retire with a little promotion when this war is over...." here he stopped speaking and glared at Chips, who panted in an impish-looking grin back at him.

"Yes, sir. Is there anything else, sir?"

The colonel cleared his throat, "Ah, yes, one more thing. We have a new K-9 joining the unit. Should be arriving this afternoon. Sergeant Hart can't be here so I'd like you to show them around. I don't recall the dog's name but the soldier's name is Campbell."

Rowell and Chips left the colonel's tent and made their way back to camp. "Can you believe it, Chips? We've been chosen to stand guard at the big war meeting. I've heard rumors that *Winston Churchill* is coming. He's the *Prime Minister of Great Britain.*"

Chips proudly pranced in circles around Rowell with his tail held high like a flag waving in the breeze.

When they got back to their tent there was even more excitement. The new K-9 and his human partner had arrived. Chips recognized both of them immediately from the War Dog Training Center. It was the sensitive-looking shepherd named Jake with the soft-spoken handler he had seen the first day at camp.

"I'm John Rowell and this is Chips. Sergeant Hart couldn't be here to welcome you, so the Colonel asked us to show you around."

"The Colonel did that? Gee, we sure would appreciate it, wouldn't we Jake?" the redheaded soldier said as he shook Rowell's hand.

Chips and Jake also made their introductions by sniffing each other from nose to tail. Chips could sense the slender shepherd was smart but quiet and reserved by nature.

"Both Jake and I took sick back at the port in Virginia, pneumonia they said it was," Campbell explained. "We spent nearly a month in the infirmary and missed out on getting here for all the action. I couldn't see Jake for most of that time either. Poor guy thought I'd abandoned him." He bent over and affectionately patted Jake on the head. Chips knew immediately they shared a great affection and devotion toward each other.

At that moment Torpedo, one of the puppies from Mena's litter, bounded up to greet them.

"Hold on there, young fellow," Rowell said grabbing him by the collar.

Jake was uncertain of the frisky pup's intentions and stiffened as Torpedo jumped up and gave him a playful nip on the ear.

"Torpedo's become the platoon's *mascot* ever since we shipped his mother, Mena, and the rest of her pups back to the States. We thought they'd be safer there and get the proper training at the War Dog Training Center, but we just couldn't part with this guy. He's going to be some tough soldier, I'd say."

All of this was a sore point for Chips. He missed Mena terribly and thought Torpedo a poor substitute. The puppy could make an enormous pest of himself. He broke free from his tie-out at least once a week and had to be fetched back, and he was frequently found chewing on perfectly good socks and boots. But worst of all, Torpedo had on more than one occasion eaten some of Chips's precious rations. This was an infraction the big dog couldn't forgive or forget.

★　　★　　★

Much of the following three days were spent training for the upcoming summit meeting. Pal and Jake had also been assigned to work as sentries. When the morning arrived for them to report for duty both K-9's and their handlers were confident of doing a good job.

"You and Chips will be stationed at the top of the front steps," Sergeant Hart said when he gave Rowell his orders. "You're to stand guard while the *MP's* check the paperwork for every person entering the building."

"Yes, sir." Rowell saluted.

The building where the meeting was being held was on a hill overlooking the city of Casablanca. From the top steps you could see for miles out over the palm trees and colorful tile roofs all the way to the sea.

At the top of the front steps to the building, Chips listened to the sound of voices and traffic coming from the narrow streets and shopping bazaars. He sat at attention next to Rowell's leg and breathed in the aromatic scents from the market place in the city below them. Never before had Chips detected so many different mouth-watering smells.

Sentry work proved rather dull. Approximately every thirty minutes he and Rowell would march across the wide veranda to a different viewing point. Occasionally, they would catch glimpses of Pal and Jake who were posted at the back and sides of the massive white building. Although they stood under the shelter of a small canopy, the glaring African sun penetrated through the thin canvas and reflected off the surrounding buildings. Hot and bored, Chips watched at attention as official-looking persons and soldiers climbed up the long staircase and the MP's checked one set of papers after another.

Many of the visitors were dressed in uniforms blazoned with gold and silver medals. All of the soldiers saluted these men. There were also visitors who came wearing fancy clothes like the suits Father wore to church. One elderly gentleman arrived accompanied by an entourage of reporters with flashing cameras. He waved as he walked passed, and Chips caught the strong odor of cigar smoke. Father did not ordinarily smoke cigars but their neighbor Mr. Rand had brought one to the house the day after Mrs. Rand had a new baby. Father said it was the best Cuban cigar he'd ever had.

"Chips," Rowell said excitedly after the portly man was out of earshot, "That was Winston Churchill, the Prime Minister of Great Britain."

Chips politely wagged his tail in response to his partner's enthusiasm. The truth was he didn't particularly care for the aroma of cigars. Besides, Chips's attention had been diverted by someone else. At the base of the steps was a large black convertible with a small American flag tied to the front. What had alerted the sensitive dog was the unusual-sounding voice coming from the car. What's more, it was a friendly voice Chips recognized as having heard many times before. It was the man Mother, Father, and the children often listened to on the radio.

"Thank you, gentlemen," the man spoke to a large group of news reporters, "I'm pleased to be here in Casablanca, and I'm hopeful great strides will be made to bring this war a rapid and just end." The man continued to speak as he was helped up the stairs and into a waiting wheel chair.

"Can you believe it, Chips?" Rowell proudly whispered. "We're guarding the President of the United States. Wait until I write them back home. No one will believe it!"

Roosevelt turned to them as he passed and smiled. "That's a terrific-looking K-9 partner you have with you, Private. Is this one of our Dogs for Defense recruits I've heard so much about?"

"Yes, sir, I mean, yes, Mr. President, sir," Rowell stammered. He was so flabbergasted Roosevelt had stopped to speak with them he couldn't get the words out properly.

"I know a little about dogs but I can't place his breed."

"He's a husky-shepherd-collie mix, sir."

"Yes, I can see he has a husky's look about him. What's his name?"

"Chip, I mean Chips," Rowell stuttered again.

"A fine-looking dog. Carry on, Private," Roosevelt said, saluting them with a smile.

As Rowell returned the salute Chips leapt forward toward the President and let out a joyful bark. Seeing the human behind the voice of the *fireside chats* was not good enough for the eager dog. He desperately wanted to touch and sniff the man who reminded him of *home*. The person who could reassure him that Mother, Father, and the children were not really so far away.

"Chips!" Rowell shouted, reining him back on his leash.

The colonel, who had been close by heard the commotion. He came running just in time to see Chips let out a terrific howl as he tried to lunge toward President Roosevelt one more time before two MP's helped Rowell drag him away. When Rowell looked back he was certain the colonel was going to faint.

★　★　★

The Casablanca Conference lasted for more than a week as the heads of the Allied forces debated the best way to win the war. In the end, it was decided that the next great battle assault would take place in Sicily— a small rocky island off the southern coast of Italy. Over two thousand vessels and half a million soldiers, sailors, and airmen would take part in the invasion against the Nazis and Fascists, two of the enemy Axis powers. Strangely, the mission was code-named Operation Husky.

CHAPTER 12

OPERATION HUSKY

"I didn't know you could get storms like this in the Mediterranean Sea in July," Campbell said and coughed nervously. He wrapped his *regulation* Army cape more snugly around his shoulders.

Rowell nodded in agreement. Both men huddled together with Chips and Jake close at their sides as the wind whipped across the deck of their troop transport ship.

"This is one heck of a night for a landing," Campbell added.

Rowell looked out into the black sea. "Yes, but no one will ever suspect an invasion tonight in these gale winds."

Both men looked up as a *sortie of planes* flew low overhead carrying *paratroopers* poised to jump out once they reached enemy territory. They saluted the *formation*, and in their hearts said a small prayer for the brave soldiers.

Chips and Jake also watched the planes as they tried to hold their course in the strong wind. Both dogs knew something important was about to happen. They knew this from the tone in the men's voices as they talked over their battle plans, they knew from the way the young soldiers meticulously cleaned their guns and checked and re-checked their equipment, but most of all Chips and Jake understood the gravity of their approaching mission from the way their humans grew quiet and reflective as the important day drew near.

"A lot of the men and dogs have been seasick," Campbell said.

"After a night like tonight, I think most of them will be happy to put their feet on solid ground, war or no war." Rowell noticed Campbell looked pale and unwell himself. "Maybe you should see if they have anything to give you in the sickbay. It's going to be a rough night."

As they talked, the colonel approached. "Better give your gear one last check," he said. "Pack up well. I expect we'll lose a few landing boats in these *Mussolini winds*."

Campbell looked even paler as the colonel removed his gold pocket watch, checked the time, and walked away, calmly whistling to himself.

Just then Torpedo trotted up to Jake and swiped him on the nose with his paw. At ten months the young pup already stood an inch taller than the older dog. Jake stoically tolerated the puppy's mauling. Chips, however, regarded the ill-mannered start-up with disdain, and Torpedo was careful to keep his distance from the giant canine.

"Don't worry, old boy. He'll be trained and ready to join us before you know it," Rowell said. He understood nearly everything about Chips except for his feelings of dislike toward Torpedo.

The puppy wagged his tail and gave Rowell's hand a friendly lick.

Chips's low growl was lost in the sound of the howling wind.

The ship's loudspeaker was also impossible to decipher in the fierce weather, and Sergeant Hart called out orders as he made his way along the deck. "Pal, Jake, Scout, Watch, and Chips will go with the first group. I'm holding the rest of the dogs back until we know what kind of resistance we get from the enemy. Best prepare your K-9's for landing!"

The men and dogs quickly moved into position to board one of the Higgins boats. Chips sensed the nervousness of the soldiers. Although they had practiced *maneuvers* for the landing many times, he knew this time would be different.

Once they were down in the small boats the stormy sea was even more frightening than from the deck of the ship. The waves were enormous and threatened to swamp them. Within minutes from leaving the troop ship the fog and rain erased all visibility and the giant carrier eerily disappeared.

Rowell drew his rain poncho over both himself and Chips. The mask-faced dog pushed his nose out from under the protection to sniff the air. He could detect no scent of land as the prevailing winds were moving toward the beachhead. Suddenly, out of the mist, the mountainous outline of Sicily loomed in front of them.

Within moments the dark sky was streaked with red flares and intense *anti-aircraft fire*. Flashes of light followed by thunderous explosions silhouetted the approaching shore. From the distance the entire beach appeared aflame, like a giant campfire. As they drew closer to the beach Chips heard showers of bullets spraying the water around their boat. A voice a few feet away from where he and Rowell sat shouted he'd been hit, and two men moved forward to help the wounded soldier. Before they had reached land the men jumped out, and using the landing boat as a kind of shield, struggled through the foaming surf to the shore. Small white -caps washed over Chips's head as he choked and paddled his way toward land.

"Down!" Rowell signaled when they reached the beach.

The gunfire was so heavy they had to flatten their bodies against the hard sand. Chips crouched and crawled along next to his companion, scraping his belly on pebbles and small pieces of broken seashells. With each new blast the young soldier protectively threw his arm over Chips. The stinging sand blew into the dog's eyes and filled his nostrils until he could no longer see or smell in any direction.

"Go fast," Rowell instructed as American bombs landed perilously close to where they crawled. *"Friendly fire's* just as deadly as enemy guns!"

Chips's body vibrated and his head ached from the repeated explosions of bombs and grenades. The world was engulfed in smoke and flames. When Chips and Rowell could advance no farther, they took cover behind a jeep that had been rolled on its side and abandoned.

Feeling sick, Rowell put his arms over his head and lay face down on the sand. A shell ripped into the beach near to them. Chips pulled on the sleeve of his partner's uniform but he wouldn't move. Seeing that his efforts were hopeless, the big dog began furiously digging a kind of *foxhole*. When he was satisfied that it was both wide and deep enough he grabbed the back Rowell's helmet with his teeth and tugged. This jerking action snapped the dazed soldier to his senses and he gratefully rolled into the protective hole.

It seemed like hours passed before the shelling and firing finally stopped. The Fascists, outnumbered and outmaneuvered by American soldiers, retreated back. Rowell, now fully recovered, quickly located Sergeant Hart and several other soldiers from their platoon who had gathered near a cluster of boulders.

Hart smiled to see that Rowell and Chips were safe. "We can take a breather here before we push on," he said.

The men relaxed on some scattered rocks. Chips, exhausted from crawling nearly a mile, lay down next to Rowell. The salt water, sand, and smoke were still stinging his eyes and throat. Seeing Chips's discomfort, Rowell took out his canteen to wash out the weary dog's eyes and give him a drink.

The soldiers immediately began talking about their next move inland from the beach.

"Anybody seen Campbell or Cobbs?" Rowell asked.

Chips's ears pricked forward at the sound of their names.

"I directed them to scout the area north of the beachhead," Hart responded. He could see Rowell was worried about his friends. "We'll do a *reconnaissance* along the south side and meet up with them later to set up camp."

"Which way do we head now, Sergeant?"

Hart pointed to a small concrete hut in the distance, "Over by that *pillbox* looks like the best route. We'll rest here first, then we'll check it out to see if the enemy left any presents behind. Sometimes those *machine gun nests* are filled with abandoned *ammo*," he added.

Chips was enjoying his drink of water almost as much as he would have enjoyed a juicy steak. Yet, when he glanced in the direction the sergeant had pointed, an unexplainable foreboding sensation overcame him, and he fixed his gaze on the concrete hut. There was something about it he didn't like.

Chips had seen these small buildings before during practice maneuvers. He knew they were used to house machine guns. He'd never paid much attention to them during drills, but this one gave him an uneasy feeling that permeated his entire body. He carefully sniffed the air, but the wind was moving away from him and he detected no suspicious scents. Most canines are blessed with superior senses but a few, like Chips, are endowed with something more: an intuitive sixth sense.

Chips stood up and took a few slow but deliberate steps toward the hut. His ears were cocked forward and the muscles in his body rippled in readiness.

"What is it, fellow?" Rowell asked as he watched

his partner's body tense and stiffen. "What do you see?" Then he followed Chips's trail of vision. "The pillbox!" he gasped.

As Rowell spoke a blast of machine gun fire sprayed bullets around them. Everyone dove for cover—everyone except Chips. Before Rowell could stop him, the fearless war dog streaked across the open ground and into the concrete hut.

Chips heard a popping noise and felt something hot sear the top of his head. Then he felt another bullet graze his shoulder but he kept going. The small room was dark and smelled of strong tobacco. Chips paused for a second to adjust his eyes to the dim light. His gaze fell on a cluster of enemy soldiers hunched together, all with a look of shock on their faces at seeing the wolf-like dog looming over them. Only the gunner turned and defiantly stared at him.

Chips didn't hesitate. With one great leap he knocked the gunner to the ground, pinning him by the neck. Chips closed his jaws over the man's jugular. It was the way his ancestors had killed their prey in the wild for thousands of years. Chips could feel the man's blood pulsating through his veins. Another fraction of an inch and his fangs would pierce the thin layer of skin. Yet something stopped him. Perhaps it was his training or maybe he was simply too kind to end this stranger's life. Steadfastly, Chips held his captive and waited for Rowell.

No one, including Rowell, could believe the scene inside the machine gun nest. Chips was holding onto the throat of the gunner, and five terrified Fascist soldiers had their hands raised in surrender.

"Release," Rowell commanded. Chips slowly pulled away from the trembling soldier. That's when Rowell saw blood trickling down his companion's head and shoulder.

The men wound bandages over Chips's wounds to stop the bleeding, and wrapped him in a canvas tarp to keep him warm until they could find a *medic.*

★　★　★

"Your dog was lucky those bullets only grazed him," said the *field surgeon* who attended to Chips's wounds. "And they don't appear to have slowed him down one bit either. I'd say he's ready for more combat." The doctor smiled and shook his head.

Rowell proudly watched as his partner strutted out of the *MASH* tent wagging his tail. He was wearing a large white bandage wrapped like a turban around his head. Another one wound around his left shoulder.

"Chips, you look like a real war hero now," Rowell laughed.

When they were finally reunited with the rest of their unit it was growing dark.

Campbell greeted them with open arms. "Jake and I were sure worried about you," he said. "You and Chips have orders to go back out with the night patrol. That's if Chips is ready to go back to work," he added.

"Ready?" Rowell grinned as Chips pranced around him and cheerfully barked. "I'd say we're both ready for our next mission."

"Hart says the area is still infested with Fascists, so

watch your step. Pal and Cobbs took the first shift. Jake and I will follow after you."

"Thanks for the warning and stay safe yourself," he said. Chips was standing next to Jake and gave the gentle dog a friendly nuzzle goodbye.

Chips knew patrol work was different from sentry work. He understood absolute silence was necessary to maintain the element of surprise should they happen upon the enemy. The strong winds of the previous night had died down and the soft Mediterranean air was almost balmy. Chips listened to the sound of crickets and the occasional night call of sea birds flying overhead. They had walked for nearly a mile over rocky terrain when he detected a different kind of sound. It was the crunching of booted footsteps. Chips knew by scent these were not American soldiers. The hackles along his back bristled and he froze on the spot.

Rowell, seeing Chips alert, motioned for the other two men with him to get down low behind some bushes and take cover.

Chips continued to listen to the foreign voices of the approaching soldiers. He could tell there were a lot of them, possibly as many as nine or ten. Worried, he looked up at his partner.

Rowell read the concern in Chips's eyes. "Stay," he silently signaled with his hand.

It took all of Chips's self control to hold himself back, but he knew this time he had to obey his orders. He crouched low on his haunches, tensed and ready.

The Americans waited in the darkness until the Fascist soldiers were almost on top of them.

"Halt!" shouted Rowell. "Drop your guns. You're surrounded."

Surprised, the men stopped in their tracks. Rowell and the other two Americans nervously stepped out of the shadows and into the moonlight with their guns pointed. But the enemy soldiers barely noticed them. Their eyes were riveted to the giant fang-bared canine with a white turban on its head. Chips glared at them and let out a deep resonant growl. They immediately dropped their rifles and surrendered.

Later that night, back at camp, the soldiers toasted Chips as the best and bravest war dog in the entire United States Army.

CHAPTER 13

FOLLOWING THE RULES

"**I** hear some top brass want to give your mutt the *Silver Star* and the *Purple Heart* for taking out that machine gun nest and being wounded in action," the colonel said several weeks later. "Let me remind you, Private Rowell, Chips disobeyed a fundamental rule when he broke away from you."

"Yes, sir," Rowell answered.

"But sir, with all due respect," Sergeant Hart interrupted, "if Chips hadn't attacked that pillbox in Sicily my men and I could have all been killed. Not to mention he assisted in the surrender of ten enemy soldiers while out on patrol later that very same night."

Chips listened attentively and thumped his tail every time he heard his name spoken.

"Rules, men, are what this military runs on. We can't reward a soldier or a dog for breaking them no matter what the outcome. Besides, even if Chips is awarded the *Purple Heart* and the *Silver Star* there are plenty of folks back in the States who believe these honors are meant for humans, not for K-9's. There will be an outcry over this!"

"It doesn't seem fair, Colonel," Hart replied. "Chips and the other dogs risk their lives in this war every day. There isn't a K-9 in this unit that wouldn't lay down his life for the men. They deserve some kind of recognition."

"Well, maybe some day they'll get that recognition." The colonel paused for a moment as if to reflect on Hart's words but then continued. "Right now I have more important business to attend to than war dogs getting medals. I've received word *General Eisenhower* plans to visit our troops here in Italy. I expect everyone to be prepared. And that means no shenanigans!"

Rowell saluted the colonel and turned to leave with Chips but Sergeant Hart lingered behind.

"Go ahead without me, Rowell," the sergeant instructed. "I have something of a private nature I need to discuss with the colonel."

★ ★ ★

When Rowell and Chips arrived back in their tent there was a package wrapped in brown paper with a familiar child's handwriting waiting for them.

"Looks like the girls have been baking more cookies," Rowell said as he carefully undid the wrapping. "And here's a note from Mother."

Chips obediently sat down and listened attentively as his partner read the words from home.

"It says: *Dear Chips and Private Rowell, We've been reading about your brave acts in all the newspapers. We're so proud of both of you for capturing those enemy soldiers. Tell Chips we'll give him the biggest roast beef dinner he's ever had when he gets home. I suspect he'd enjoy that more than any medals or honors the Army might award him.*"

At the mention of the words *roast beef* Chips let out two happy barks and gobbled up four of the home-made cookies.

"I'd say Mother is always right," Rowell said with a smile.

★   ★   ★

"Remember what the colonel said, Chips, we have to be prepared with our best behavior for the general's visit. *General Eisenhower* is the *Supreme Commander of the Allied Armies*," Rowell gave Chips's thick black and tan coat a final brushing while they waited outside the colonel's tent to meet the general.

"He's coming now," Cobbs said excitedly. All of the men and dogs stood tall at attention.

A military entourage of jeeps and motorcycles pulled up in front of the waiting troops.

"He's even taller than I thought he'd be," Campbell whispered.

The soldiers and dogs watched the lanky, energetic man briskly approach them while a group of high-ranking military officers and news reporters jockeyed to keep pace.

"Get ready, Chips," Rowell said and unconsciously tightened his grip on Chips's leash.

The alert and well-trained war dog felt his partner's body tense as the strange man approached, and he readied himself to do the right thing.

The general paused a few feet away from them. "Which one is the dog Chips I've heard so much about?" he asked.

"General, it's my pleasure to introduce Private John Rowell and his K-9 Brand 11A," the colonel said using Chips's official serial number. He then signaled for Rowell and Chips to step forward.

The general smiled. "I hear your dog has performed heroically, Private."

"Yes, thank you, sir," Rowell said nervously.

Sensing his friend's uneasiness, Chips grew even more suspicious of the tall stranger.

"He's a fine-looking soldier," Eisenhower said and he reached out his hand to give Chips a friendly pat on the head.

That's when Chips bit him!

"*OUCH!*" the general exclaimed jumping back.

"General Eisenhower, are you hurt?" an aide called out as he rushed to his commander's side.

"I'm fine, it's just a scratch," Eisenhower said, recovering quickly. "But the colonel doesn't look well."

"I, I...." stuttered the colonel. All eyes turned toward him. The color had drained from his face.

"I should have known better," Eisenhower said. "I should have remembered a war dog is trained not to trust strangers. Chips was only doing his job and following the rules. That's what I call a good soldier. Now there's a fine story for you folks to send back home, gentlemen," he added, turning to the news reporters.

Everyone, except the colonel, laughed and nodded in agreement.

CHAPTER 14

MESSENGER DOG

M ore than a year passed. It was the bitter December of 1944 when Chips and Rowell arrived with their platoon in central France. The Army was growing weary. There were fuel and ammunition shortages all along the front, and although the Nazis were losing ground, they put up a fierce struggle to defend their German homeland as the Allied soldiers pushed closer to its borders.

★　★　★

"What's the name of this town?" Cobbs shivered as he warmed his hands over a small fire.

"Trier," Rowell said without looking up. He was drying his socks over the same flame, and since he had singed several in this manner he didn't want to ruin these, his last good pair. When they weren't crouched in foxholes or searching bombed-out buildings looking for

Nazi snipers, they were trying to stay dry and avoid frostbite.

"I don't see how the dogs withstand this cold," Cobbs said as he rubbed Pal's pads between his palms.

Rowell put his socks aside and glanced over at Chips who was meticulously grooming his front paws. "Chips wasn't much more than a pup when he joined the Army. Now he's a seasoned old soldier, aren't you fellow?"

The giant dog looked up devotedly at his partner. Although his eyes were alert they showed the strain of long months of battle fatigue. Chips gathered himself up and slowly walked to Rowell. The soldier ran his hand down his back and frowned as he felt the dog's ribs beginning to protrude under his thick winter coat.

At that moment, Torpedo bounded into the tent ahead of Sergeant Hart. Although the men made attempts to train Mena's frisky son, they were often distracted by the business of war. The result was that Torpedo was sometimes an unruly and rambunctious dog.

Hart spoke directly to Rowell. "We have a problem. Last night's patrol hasn't returned. They should have been back hours ago. We've lost all radio contact. I need you to conduct a search. Two men from B Company have been assigned to go with you."

Rowell and Cobbs looked at each other with concern.

"Campbell and Jake did the midnight watch," Rowell said.

Chips empathetically whimpered and walked to the

opening of the tent.

"Better get going. No telling what could have happened to them," Hart said, shaking his head. "These woods are crawling with Nazis."

At this Cobbs started for his gun but Hart held up his hand to stop him. "No. You and Pal need to rest."

"But Sergeant...."

"Next time," Hart said and abruptly left.

Chips watched Rowell reach for his rifle. Without hesitation he retrieved his working collar from the pack where it was kept and dropped it at his partner's feet.

"You know we have an important job to do, don't you?" Rowell couldn't help but smile as he fastened the well-worn leather collar around Chips's neck. They'd been together nearly every hour of every day for more than two years. It never ceased to amaze him that Chips not only anticipated his actions but often read his innermost thoughts. "We have to find Jake and Campbell," he said.

Chips stared into Rowell's eyes for a moment as if calculating the severity of their mission, then wagged his tail to say he was ready.

As soon as the two men from B Company arrived, they set off.

Chips walked in front of the men. He alternated between scenting the air and sniffing the ground for clues to the whereabouts of Jake and Campbell. It wasn't long before his keen nose discovered their scent and followed it until he reached a thicket of brambles about a mile from camp. Here, he detected the odor of many other men, possibly as many as twenty enemy soldiers.

Chips knew Campbell and Jake were in trouble and he knew he had to find them quickly.

Suddenly Chips felt a nip on his ear. He reeled around to face Torpedo playfully wagging his tail to entice him into a game of chase and tumble. Chips had been so intent on following Jake and Campbell's scent he had failed to detect either the sound or scent of Torpedo trailing him.

"Where did you come from?" exclaimed Rowell, who hadn't seen the renegade dog approaching either. "Looks like he broke his tie-out again."

Chips looked at his partner and then at Torpedo.

"It's too late to take him back. He'll have to come with us."

Chips, ignoring the young dog, set off at a fast trot.

The gray sky closed in around them and a heavy snow began to fall. Every time Chips paused to look up and sniff the air he had to blink icy flakes from his eyes. The visibility lessened, and soon the men were completely dependent upon the dogs to lead them through the ghostly woods and fields.

"I sure hope these critters know where they're taking us," one of the soldiers commented as he stumbled over a log.

"We must be behind enemy lines by now," his partner said, looking nervously in all directions. "Maybe we should radio back to camp."

"Yeah, too bad I haven't been able to get a radio signal for the last two miles."

"We better not be lost," his partner said and began fumbling through his pack for his compass.

"Don't worry about finding the way back. We've been on hundreds of patrols and Chips has never been lost yet," Rowell reassured them.

Yet even as he spoke he too was growing concerned. Why, he thought, would Jake and Campbell have wandered so far away? The men were right. They had crossed *no man's land* and were now deep into enemy territory. If Campbell and Jake had come this far he knew they must be in bad trouble. But as Rowell watched Chips confidently forge ahead in the blinding snow he trusted they were on the right path.

The closer Chips got to his goal the faster he went. Torpedo, thinking it all a great game, happily loped along at his side. They quickly wove through a thick forest of oak and chestnut trees. Unexpectedly, Chips stopped at the top of a steep cliff and alerted. Torpedo stood quietly next to him.

"Nazis," Rowell whispered to the other men and motioned for them to get low behind some boulders.

"Where?"

Rowell pointed down into the mist-filled ravine.

"But we can't see a bloody thing in this snow. How can you be sure?"

"We'd better keep our cover and wait. They must have scouts posted," Rowell said, ignoring the soldier's doubt. He couldn't see the enemy either but he trusted Chips's canine abilities and uncanny instinct better than his own eyes.

The men and dogs remained hidden behind the outcropping of rocks. Nearly three hours passed in the freezing cold before the snow tapered to a stop and the mist lifted. Rowell slowly crawled out on his belly to survey the situation. When he looked through his binoculars he couldn't believe his eyes. Several dozen Nazi soldiers were camped at the foot of the ravine. Handcuffed under a tarp was a thin, redheaded American soldier. It was Campbell. Jake was nowhere in sight.

"What should we do?" whispered one of the men. "There're too many of them for us to fight."

"I say we go back to camp and get *reinforcements*," his buddy answered.

"But they might move their camp," Rowell said. "They must have realized we were moving in on them when they caught Campbell. There's only one thing to do, and that's to send Chips back for help."

The two men vehemently shook their heads *NO*.

"Your dog has to show us how to get back to camp. What if he gets lost, or he can't lead the guys to us?"

Rowell thought for a moment. They were right. Although Chips had often run small errands around camp carrying messages and packages he had never traveled long distances alone. He wasn't trained to be a *messenger dog*. Rowell wasn't even certain Chips would go without him, but he knew this was their only hope of rescuing Campbell. "Chips will do it," he said finally. "It'll take too long for us to hike back." He took a pencil and piece of paper out of his knapsack and wrote a message to Sergeant Hart. Then he took a piece of cord out of his pocket and carefully tied the note to Chips's collar. "Take this to Sergeant Hart, boy. Go home," Rowell whispered.

Home....

Chips ran ten paces then stopped to wait for Rowell to follow.

"I'm not coming with you this time. You'll go faster without me."

Chips continued to look inquisitively at his partner. He never went anywhere without Rowell and he didn't understand why he couldn't be with him now.

"Go *HOME*," Rowell repeated in a stern whisper.

This time Chips understood his partner's command to go it alone. Reluctantly, he turned and headed back in the direction of camp. Torpedo followed closely at his heels.

The snow had covered their earlier tracks but there was plenty of scent left for the dogs to retrace their earlier path. What's more, Chips had an infallible sense of direction. Silently, they made their way through thick forests and across open meadows, undisturbed and undetected.

When they were within a few miles of their destination Chips paused to drink from a partially frozen stream. Torpedo drank too. Chips finished first and stood alertly along the stream bank. His time in the Army had taught him to never let his guard down and to be ready for any kind of danger. As Chips stood and waited he grew uneasy. His keen intuition told him something was not right about this place. He pawed at the frozen ground and growled at Torpedo to hurry him along.

Unfortunately, nothing could rush Torpedo. Whether it was mealtime or war maneuvers the overgrown puppy did things at his own pace. Now he completely ignored Chips's warning and even went so far as to roll around in the fresh snow and playfully chomp on pieces of ice.

Chips, growing more concerned by the minute, turned to leave, and as he did he caught the faint scent of a Nazi soldier on the wind. He ran forward several paces and turned to encourage Torpedo to follow, but his silly and stubborn companion was still dawdling at the stream. Chips paused. His desire to protect the younger dog overcame his impulse to flee, and in that moment of hesitation the enemy fired his gun.

The bullet grazed Chips's side. He staggered and regained his balance. Torpedo looked confused and frightened. Chips let out a sharp bark for him to follow. Then, like the wolf that protects the location of the pack from its enemies, Chips turned and galloped in the opposite direction of the camp.

The soldier aimed his gun but the dogs instinctively ran in zigzagged fashion, and the shots missed their mark. Just when Chips was certain they had outrun their assailant they came to a deep ravine. It was too sheer and rocky to climb down, so their only choice was to jump over it. Ordinarily Chips would have had no trouble leaping across the eight-foot chasm, but the months of war and battle wounds had taken a toll on the powerful canine. He landed awkwardly and tumbled forward. Torpedo followed and made the jump easily. He waited for the older dog to get up. Chips struggled to stand but he winced in pain as his front left leg collapsed beneath him.

When the Nazi appeared on the other side of the cliff he smiled to see the big dog injured and unable to run. Torpedo, sensing Chips's plight, stood protectively in front of him. He held his tail high and bristled his fur to appear larger and more threatening. His black eyes narrowed as he coldly stared at the gloating soldier. The man raised his gun to his shoulder and fixed Chips in its *sights,* but only silence followed. The gun was out of bullets. Torpedo lowered his head and hunched his shoulders the way dogs do when they stalk their prey. Curling back his lips to show his large fangs, he growled and took several threatening steps toward the soldier. The Nazi turned and fled.

Torpedo prodded Chips with his nose for him to get up and join him. Chips struggled to his legs and limped to the edge of the ravine. Torpedo leapt gracefully across and barked in encouragement for him to follow. But Chips knew there was no way he could make the jump to the other side. Instead he lay down and sighed. Torpedo softly whimpered and reluctantly set off toward camp alone.

★　★　★

"What's this?" Sergeant Hart said when he saw Cobbs approaching with the exhausted Torpedo trailing behind him.

"It's the second time he's broken loose this week, Sergeant. Maybe we should ship him back to the states. He's nothing but trouble."

"I'd hate to lose you to the Nazis now," Hart said as

he took hold of Torpedo's collar. Then he looked more closely at the bedraggled dog and motioned to Cobbs. "Look here, he's got burrs and briars stuck all over him and his paws are pretty cut up." Hart was thoughtful for a moment. "You don't suppose he followed Rowell and the others?"

"Maybe, but where's Rowell now?"

"That's what I'd like to know. First Campbell and Jake disappear, and now Rowell and Chips are gone. I'm going out to look for them myself." Hart looked into Torpedo's eyes. "I bet you know where they are, don't you, fellow? Take us to Chips. Go find Chips."

At this Torpedo barked excitedly and backed away from the two men. Then he turned and ran a few paces and turned and barked again.

"He wants us to follow him," Sergeant Hart said, and he quickly called for reinforcements.

★　★　★

Chips opened his eyes. He had been dreaming about his old home. The place he had known before he had come to live with Rowell and the soldiers. But now he needed to get back to camp and find Sergeant Hart. These were Rowell's last orders. Carefully, he stood and placed his weight on his left leg. He winced in pain. Chips began limping along the edge of the ravine. Finally, he found a spot that was narrow enough to safely jump over on three legs. Chips had gone a short distance when he discovered the unmistakable scent of blood on the ground. It was Jake's!

★ ★ ★

When Hart, Cobbs, and the others arrived at the ravine where Torpedo had left Chips the big dog was gone. Torpedo circled the area until he found a clue to the direction his friend had taken. He easily detected Chips's trail. With his nose to the ground, Torpedo led the men another mile to a deserted stone barn. Hart gave the signal to approach slowly. Torpedo, however, was not so cautious and dashed headlong for the broken-down building. When Hart and the others arrived they found both Torpedo and Chips standing over Jake's limp body.

"Quick!" Hart shouted. "Jake's been shot." He knelt down beside the wounded war dog and felt the hole a bullet had made when it punctured his side. "He's alive," he added with relief. "The bullet must have just missed his heart and lungs."

Chips turned and limped toward the door. Now that Sergeant Hart had arrived to take care of Jake his only thought was to get back to Rowell.

"Sergeant, Chips is injured too," Cobbs called out.

Hart examined him. "His leg isn't broken but it's badly sprained. We can make stretchers out of our jackets and carry both dogs back to camp."

"What do you think happened to Campbell, Rowell, and the others?"

Then Hart saw the note attached to Chips's collar and tore it open. "It's from Rowell. They've stumbled onto a nest of a couple of dozen Nazis who are holding Campbell captive. He says Chips will lead us back to them."

Hearing Rowell's name, Chips's eyes lit up and he happily wagged his tail and barked.

"Sorry, old boy, I can't let you go. Not on that leg."

"What'll we do?"

Hart looked from Chips to the younger dog. "Torpedo will have to lead us to them. He led us to Chips. Now he can help us find Rowell."

Chips barked in protest.

"I know you think Torpedo isn't ready for this yet, Chips, but he's had you for a teacher. In the end that's the best training any war dog can ever hope to get."

★   ★   ★

"I never thought I'd see Jake again," Campbell said to the group of soldiers who gathered around to hear him tell the story of his capture for the third or fourth time. "We were surrounded by Nazis. One of them snuck up behind us. Jake took the bullet that was meant for me and then tracked us as far as that stone barn where he collapsed." Tears filled Campbell's eyes as he spoke of his partner's bravery. "Jake saved my life and now he's struggling for his own."

"The doc says he'll be fine with some rest," Sergeant Hart reassured him.

"When this war's over I'm going to take Jake home to live out the rest of his days with me. Captain Hill, the vet at Front Royal said his own family never took proper care of him. He said poor Jake was half-starved when he came into the Army. Jake deserves the best."

"It looks like you'll be leaving sooner than you thought, Campbell," the colonel announced. He had arrived in time to overhear the end of Campbell's story. "I've just received orders for you and Jake to ship home."

"That's great news!" Rowell exclaimed, patting Campbell on the back. Hart, Cobbs, and the others congratulated him too.

"Oh yes, I've also received orders for Chips to be transferred to the *rear*. He'll do a few months of sentry work at a *POW* camp before he's *discharged*," the colonel added.

"The rear? Discharged?" Rowell repeated with disbelief. "You mean we're going home?"

"I said Chips is going to be sent back. I didn't say anything about you."

"But...I wouldn't be much of a soldier without Chips. Chips and I are a team, sir."

"This is the Army, Rowell. We don't have time for sentimentality. You'll be assigned another war dog."

"But Colonel...." Rowell protested.

The colonel turned on his heel and started to walk away when Hart stopped him.

"What about the medals, Colonel? Remember? The medals we spoke about?"

"Yes, I recall our conversation." The colonel removed his watch from his pocket and examined it. "Have your platoon outside my tent at *2200 hours* sharp." Then he snapped the watch shut and walked away, muttering to himself about rules and regulations.

"What's all this about medals?" Rowell asked after the colonel was out of earshot.

"Just a promise the old man made to me a long time ago. You'll find out soon enough."

★　★　★

At *2200 hours* the soldiers gathered outside the colonel's tent.

"I realize many of you men were upset when the Army revoked Chips's *Purple Heart* and *Silver Star*." The colonel paused and cleared his throat. "While I'm in agreement that an animal shouldn't receive awards meant for human soldiers, and don't believe that such honors should be given when rules are disobeyed, I do believe Chips's heroism should be commended. To this end I would like to present him with an award."

The colonel held up a ribbon. On it was an arrowhead representing the assault landing Chips had participated in during the invasion of Sicily and eight stars—one for each battle campaign he served in during the years he had been a soldier.

All the men cheered.

Rowell stepped forward to accept the ribbon. Then he knelt down and pinned it to Chips's collar. "I know honors like this don't mean anything to you. But in my book you're the bravest and smartest dog in the whole United States Army. We've been through a lot together and I'll never forget you. You're the best friend a soldier can have. No matter where this crazy war takes me, I'll always think of you at my side."

Chips licked the tears that were streaming down Rowell's cheeks. He couldn't comprehend his partner's words but he implicitly understood the love that was in his heart.

★   ★   ★

"It's time for you to go home to your family," Rowell said as he gave Chips his final grooming. "You won't be needing this anymore," he added, removing Chips's working collar and replacing it with the one he had worn when he had first arrived at boot camp in Front Royal.

Chips wagged his tail and pawed at Rowell's knee.

"No, I can't come with you this time. But don't worry, I'll have Torpedo to look after me."

The young dog bounded up to Chips and playfully nipped his ear. Chips affectionately nuzzled him back.

Then, one by one, all of the men and K-9's said their farewells.

"It's been an honor to serve with you, Chips," Cobbs said. "Pal and I are going to miss you terribly."

When it was Sergeant Hart's turn to say good-bye, he knelt down beside the big dog and took a medal out of his pocket. It was the battle star he had received in Sicily. He carefully pinned it to Chips's collar. "You're the one who really deserves this honor, old boy. Thanks for watching out over my men and keeping them safe."

When they were finished with their farewells, Rowell placed Chips in his old crate in the back of a jeep. Chips whimpered as he watched through the small window until Rowell and the others faded out of sight.

CHAPTER 15

A STAR IN THE WINDOW

The train pulled into the little village station on a cold but clear winter morning. Six reporters and photographers accompanied Chips in his private railroad car. It was a hero's homecoming. Chips stepped off the train and blinked into the bright sunlight. Mother and Father were standing waiting for him with their friends and neighbors.

"Oh, goodness, he's even bigger than when he left," Mrs. Rand exclaimed and put her hand to her heart.

"He must have eaten the Army clean out of rations," Mrs. Larson added, laughing.

Mother knelt down and gently called to him. She held out her hand for him to examine. In one sniff all the memories of home came flooding back to Chips. Then Mother gave him a big hug.

As Mother hugged him Chips saw a young blonde-haired boy staring at him. There was something famil-iar about the child that made Chips's heart skip a beat.

It was young John. But he was no longer a small toddler. He was six, and tall and strong-looking for his age.

"Chips!" John called out. "Here, boy, come here!" It took all of five seconds for the two to reacquaint themselves. Chips wiggled from nose to tail with excitement, and could not give John enough kisses. The boy laughed until he fell over.

"Hello, Chips," Father said, scratching him behind the ears the way he always did. "It's good to have you back."

The reporters gathered around Mother and fired questions at her.

"How does it feel to have your dog home again?"

"Does he look the same to you?"

"Did the Army change him at all?"

"Except for a few battle scars and looking a bit weary from his long journey, Chips looks exactly the same," Mother answered.

"It's been reported he single-handedly captured an enemy machine gun nest and held the gunner by the throat. Are you worried he might be too vicious to be a family pet again?"

"Chips, too vicious? Heavens no," Mother laughed as she watched the giant dog and John playing together. "He's as gentle as a lamb. Besides, Chips successfully completed his *retraining* at the Front Royal War Dog Training Center. The Army has assured us he's ready to be a *civilian* again."

★ ★ ★

Later that afternoon there was more celebrating when Gail and Nan arrived home from school. They'd both grown so tall Chips barely recognized them when they came screaming through the kitchen door and smothered him with kisses.

"Slow down, girls," Mother cautioned. "Chips needs time to adjust to being a part of our family again."

That night Chips found his favorite spot near the fireplace and immediately went to sleep.

"It's almost like he was never gone," Mother commented to one of the reporters who stopped by to take photographs of the hero dog's first night at home.

"But he doesn't wag his tail as much as he did before he went to war," Gail added, frowning.

Nan nodded in agreement.

★　　★　　★

It was true. Chips was the same dog, and yet he was different. He still loved to romp and play chase with the children; he eagerly pulled John on his sled through the snow; and he was invigorated by a game of catch with his favorite old tennis ball, but something about him had changed.

"Why is Chips so serious?" Nan asked one night at dinner several weeks later. "Sometimes he even looks sad."

"I'm afraid our Mr. Chips has seen and experienced things we'll never really know or understand," Mother explained.

Gail was thoughtful. "You mean like Mr. Green the

postman? He doesn't smile as much as he did before he went to war, and when Nan and I speak to him he acts like his thoughts are a thousand miles away."

"Yes, Gail, I believe Chips must feel the same way." Then Mother hesitated for a moment. "You know, our home is also very different from the one Chips left to go into the Army. You're both older now, and busy with your own lives. Even John isn't the same boy anymore. He's away at school all day. Chips had an important job to do in the military. His days must seem very dull for him now that he's home."

"Nan and I promised we'd take him to his favorite forest when he came back from the war."

"That's a wonderful idea, girls. We can make a day of it. The lake should be frozen, and you can go skating."

The following Saturday everyone bundled into the car and headed to the forest on the outskirts of the little village.

"Look, Mother," Nan exclaimed when they arrived, "I think Chips remembers this place. He's running to all the spots he used to go to search for squirrels and rabbits." Everyone laughed to see Chips lift his head up from scenting a trail with snow covering the end of his muzzle."

"He still looks like a clown with a big black nose and giant ears," Father laughed. Chips's eyes twinkled with delight to be back in his favorite place surrounded by his family.

The girls and John enjoyed their skating. Afterwards, while the family was busy looking for fresh evergreen boughs for the fireplace mantle, Chips wandered off to rest under a fir tree on a bed of soft pine needles.

Chips closed his eyes and drifted off to sleep. He dreamed he was back in the Army with his old friends. They were all sitting together the way they used to in the evenings, around a warm campfire, talking and laughing. Everyone was there: Private Rowell, Sergeant Hart, Cobbs, Campbell, Jake, and Pal. Even Mena was there with her puppies.

Suddenly Rowell called his name, "Chips! Come Chips!"

But it wasn't his partner calling to him, it was Father.

"You had us worried for a minute," Father said when he discovered him. "But I guess if you could fight your way through half of Europe you can find your way around these small woods."

Chips stood and shook away his dream, and followed Father back to the family.

★ ★ ★

It was the first warm Saturday in April when Mother agreed to allow John to walk into the village with Chips to buy a comic book. John had been begging to take the big dog for a walk without his mother, father, or sisters to escort him.

"I want to wear my navy blue sailor's jacket so I can be a military man just like Chips."

Mother smiled at the eager boy. "Won't Chips be proud of you!"

John and Chips slowly made their way down the sidewalk toward the village. Chips obediently walked at the young boy's side. They had come to an intersection when a woman on the other side of the street grabbed her two young children and ran away in the opposite direction. John thought nothing of it and kept walking.

They had barely walked another block when a man in a car shouted out the window. "Get that monster off the street!"

When they arrived at the newspaper and comic book shop the owner stopped them at the door. "Sorry, son, your dog's not allowed in here."

"Why not?" John asked.

"I'm afraid he'll scare away my customers."

"A killer like that doesn't belong in civilized society anymore," a man said as he quickly left the store with his frightened wife.

"But Chips isn't a killer and he isn't a monster either," John stammered. "He doesn't even bite." With that the boy turned and ran home with Chips close at his side.

"Why are you crying?" Mother asked when John burst through the front door with tears streaming down both cheeks.

"It's because of Chips," Gail stated matter-of-factly. "When I took him for a walk around the block last week Mrs. Miller told her children to go inside until we were out of sight. She said we have no right bringing a vicious war dog back home."

"Why, that's ridiculous," Mother exclaimed. "Chips wouldn't hurt a mouse. I'll go have a talk with Mrs.

Miller."

"It's no use. Nobody likes Mr. Chips anymore," Nan added.

Mother looked at the children and then at Chips who lay quietly under the dining room table. His eyes had a sad and faraway look to them. *Just like Mr. Green's,* she thought. That's when Mother got an idea.

"Has the mail arrived yet?" she asked.

"No," Gail said, looking at her mother suspiciously.

"What does the mail have to do with Chips?" Nan asked.

"Oh, maybe nothing," Mother said as she disappeared out the door, and headed in the opposite direction of Mrs. Miller's house.

When Mother returned she was with Mr. Green. Chips immediately jumped up to greet his old friend. He'd seen the mailman many times since he'd returned home but he was always joyful for the opportunity to visit.

"I hear some of the village folks are giving our Mr. Chips a hard time," Mr. Green said to the children.

"Chips isn't a killer," John said, choking back more tears.

"You're right about that," Mr. Green said with a smile, and gave both John and Chips a sympathetic pat on the head.

"Why are you here?" Gail asked.

"I thought Chips could keep me company on my route today. Besides, I have something special I've been meaning to do for a long time and I think Chips can help me."

★ ★ ★

Mr. Green and Chips made their way up and down the sidewalks delivering mail. All along the route Mr. Green stopped to talk to people and to introduce Chips as his new helper. He explained that although Chips was a brave and fearless soldier, he was also a loving and gentle pet. Many people hurried away from them. "Don't worry, Chips," he said. "Folks have a hard time getting over their prejudices, but they'll come around. You just have to give them time."

When they'd finished delivering the mail Mr. Green took his new four-legged partner to a small street Chips had never visited before. The street was lined with tidy little houses. They stopped in front of one that looked identical to all of the others except for a large banner with a gold star hanging in the front window. Mr. Green looked at the house for a long time as if he wasn't certain whether he should proceed to the door or not.

"This isn't part of our mail route, Chips. This is Charlie Wilson's house. Charlie never made it home from the war. His parents decided to bury him in France with the rest of his unit. They knew it's what he would have wanted."

Chips, sensing Mr. Green's sadness, pushed his velvety muzzle into the mailman's hand to comfort him.

"I've been wanting to visit his mother for a long time, but I didn't know what to say to her. I guess I've been feeling guilty because I made it back from the war and Charlie didn't. Now that you're here I think I have the courage to pay my respects."

A pretty woman with gray hair opened the door and invited them inside. "I know how hard this must be for you," she said to Mr. Green. "You and Charlie had been friends since you were little boys. But I'm glad you're here because seeing you makes me feel closer to my son."

"I'd like you to meet a special friend of mine and Charlie's, Mrs. Wilson," Mr. Green said, and motioned to his companion.

"So this is the famous Mr. Chips," Charlie's mother exclaimed with a warm smile. "I'm pleased to make your acquaintance." She leaned down and took the paw Chips held up to her. "Charlie was so proud when he heard about your brave deeds. He wrote and told me to save the articles about you from the newspapers. See here, I was saving them for Charlie." Mrs. Wilson went to the coffee table and came back with a photo album. In it were pictures of Charlie in his uniform and three news clippings about Chips's capture of the enemy pillbox and soldiers in Italy. "I also saved the news clipping about the time you nipped General Eisenhower. I think Charlie would have had a good laugh over that one." Mrs. Wilson smiled.

Mr. Green and Chips visited with Charlie's mother until it was almost dark. Mr. Green promised to stop by often and to bring Chips with him. He said Chips was going to be his assistant until the townspeople got used to having a real war dog hero living among them. Mrs. Wilson thought it was a wonderful idea.

★　★　★

"Father, guess what?" John announced that night at dinner. "Chips has a new job. He's going to be a mailman!"

"You don't say," Father replied. "I bet he'll be very good at it."

Mother smiled and slipped a slice of roast beef under the table. Chips happily thumped his tail.

★　★　★

GLOSSARY

Aircraft carrier –   a ship designed as a floating air-
                            field and used as a base for air-
                            craft to land and take off
Air raid –   an attack by aircraft on ground
                            targets
Alert –   when a dog warns or indicates
                            the presence of something or
                            someone
Allied Forces –   alliance that included the United
                            States, Great Britain, France,
                            and Russia
Ammo –   slang for ammunition
Anti-aircraft –   any type of weapon firing at air-
                            craft from the ground
Artillery tank –   heavily armored, all terrain vehi-
                            cle with guns
Assault –   the time between the first land-
                            ing of troops and weapons and
                            the accomplishment of their mis-
                            sion
AWOL –   leaving or being absent without
                            permission
Axis Powers –   the alliance of Germany, Italy,
                            and Japan in World War II
Barracks –   military housing for soldiers
Batteries –   groups of guns, cannons, tor-
                            pedo tubes, searchlights etc. of
                            the same size, range, and caliber

	working together
Battleship –	a heavily armored warship
Battle stations –	*"man all battle stations"* all persons take positions to prepare to fight
Battle theatre –	the place of action or fighting during a war
Beachhead –	designated area along the shoreline where once it is seized and held a continuous landing of more troops and materials is possible
Bivouacking –	to make a temporary or open campsite without a tent
Blackouts –	communities turned off all house, business, and streetlights to practice in case enemy planes tried to bomb America
Boot camp –	a training camp for soldiers
Bow –	the forward end of a ship
Brand numbers –	identification numbers tattooed onto the inside of a war dog's left ear
Bridge or Captain's bridge –	a raised area from which the ship is steered and navigated
Brigade –	control two or more battalions and are often led by Colonels or Brigadier Generals
Canteen –	(1) a military club or store (2) thermos to carry water or other liquid
Cargo –	goods carried on the ships and planes

Casablanca –	a seaport in northwest Morocco and the site of the Casablanca Conference where heads of the Allied Forces met to plan war strategy
Cease-fire –	a period of truce when opposing sides stop fighting
Choke collar –	a chain link metal collar that slips over a dog's head and is used in training. This type of collar contracts when the leash is pulled (a *check*) and then releases immediately, providing a correctional signal to the dog
Civilian –	a person not in the military or the police force
Company –	contains two or more platoons and usually led by a Captain
Court-martialed –	to be taken before a military judicial court for disciplinary reasons
Cruisers –	naval vessel having high speed, a wide radius of action, and relatively large, long-range guns
Destroyers –	naval vessel of high speed armed with light, rapid-fire guns and deck torpedo tubes. Provide protection for other ships
Detachment –	troops deployed for a special purpose
Discharged –	to be dismissed from military service

Distinguished – Service Cross	an award given for extraordinary heroism
Dogs for Defense –	established in 1942, this organization developed a nationwide network of volunteers, trainers, and kennel clubs to recruit dogs for military service. During its first two years approximately 40,000 dogs were volunteered. Of these approximately 10,000 passed through the training program
Duffle Bags –	large cylinder-shaped canvas bag the soldiers and sailors used for clothing and personal items
Embarkation –	to go on board a ship or aircraft to reach a destination
Enlisted –	to enroll in the armed services
Fala –	the Roosevelt's Scottish terrier named after the President's ancestor *Murray the Outlaw of Falahill,* and nicknamed *Fala.* Fala died at age 12, and is buried in the Rose Garden at Hyde Park, Roosevelt's home along the Hudson River
Fascists –	an extreme totalitarian nationalist movement first instituted in Italy in 1922-23. The Fascists were led by the dictator Benito Mussolini (1922-1943). They were part of the Axis Powers
Fatigues –	clothing worn by soldiers when they are not doing work duty

Field desk –	a small lightweight desk used by high-ranking military officers in battle areas, camp sites, etc.
Field surgeon –	a name used for surgeons who conducted surgery in battle areas, camp sites, etc.
Fireside chats –	a name used to refer to President Roosevelt's frequent radio talks during the war
Fleet –	a group of warships under one commander-in-chief
Flight deck –	the place where aircraft lands and takes off from on an aircraft carrier
Footlockers –	a small trunk kept at the foot of a soldier's bed
Formation –	an arrangement of soldiers, troops, ships, or aircraft
Foxholes –	a hole dug into the ground for shelter during battle
Friendly fire –	ammunition, shells, bombs, etc. used by your own military or that of your allies
Frigates –	naval escort vessel or light war-ship
Front –	the foremost line of action in a battle
Gas mask –	nose and mouth covering worn by humans and dogs to protect against poisonous gases and nox-ious fumes
General – Eisenhower	US General, Supreme Commander of the

	Allied Armies, and 34th US President (1953-1961)
General – George Patton	US General and commander of the Third Army during WWII
General quarters –	*"Sound General Quarters!"* a call to battle stations for all hands
Gunboats –	a small vessel with heavy guns
Hackles –	hairs on an animal's back that rise when the animal is angry or alarmed
Hand grenades –	small bombs thrown by hand
Handler –	the person in-charge of caring for and working with a war dog
Heel –	a command to follow closely at the handler's side
Higgins boat –	designed and built by Andrew Higgins of New Orleans, these boats were 36 feet long by 10 feet wide. Half metal and half wood, they could maneuver all the way to shore, drop their front end to create a ramp, and unload guns and men in a matter seconds. These landing boats were considered instrumental in the Allies winning the war
Home front –	words used to describe America's homeland during the war and the work being done at home to fight the war overseas
Howitzer guns –	type of small cannon
Infirmary –	hospital or medical building
K-9 –	military word used for the work-

	ing dogs – a play on *canines*
Machine gun nest –	a group of machine gunners
Maneuvers –	planned and controlled movement of military personnel
Mascot –	person, animal, or thing meant to bring good luck
MASH tent –	stands for <u>M</u>obile <u>A</u>rmy <u>S</u>urgical <u>H</u>ospital – generally located close to the fighting
Medic –	medical serviceman or servicewoman
Messenger dog –	Trained to work with two handlers instead of one, and to carry messages between them
Mess hall –	military dining area
Military time –	uses a 24-hour time scale that makes AM and PM unnecessary. For example: Midnight is 0000, 1PM is 1300, and 2100 is 9PM
Minesweeper –	a ship used for clearing explosive mines from the sea
MP's –	the military maintains its own police force called <u>M</u>ilitary <u>P</u>olice
Mussolini Winds –	a nickname given to the heavy winds the American Forces had to battle in the Mediterranean. Named for the Fascist dictator (See "Fascist")
Muzzle –	(1) the projecting part of an animal's face including the nose and mouth. (2) guard put over an animal's nose and mouth to pre-

Nazis –	vent it from biting or eating member(s) of the German Nationalist Socialist party and led by Adolf Hitler (1933-1945) Part of the Axis Powers
Newsreels –	a short movie of recent events
No man's land –	the space of land between two opposing armies
Oil tankers –	large sea vessel carrying oil
Operation Husky –	code name given to Allied invasion of Sicily
Operation Torch –	code name given to Allied invasion of North Africa
Paratroopers –	soldiers deployed to parachute out of aircraft into combat areas
Patrol work –	dogs and handlers were sent out of camp base to watch a specified area
Pearl Harbor –	inlet on the south coast of the island of Oahu in Hawaii, and the site of a large US naval base
Periscope –	an instrument used by submarines to see what is happening on the surface of the water
Pillbox –	a small concrete fort or hut used to fire weapons from
Platoon –	small collection of several squads or crews and usually led by Lieutenants or a Sergeant First Class
Post –	a troop base
POW –	an enemy Prisoner Of War
Prime Minister –	chief executive of the government

Purple Heart –	oldest military decoration in the world in present use, and the first American award made available to the common soldier. It was created as the *Badge of Merit* by George Washington. It's awarded for being wounded or killed by an instrument of war in the hands of the enemy
Quarantine –	three-week period of isolation imposed on the dogs to prevent the spread of disease or infection
Quonset hut –	semi-cylinder shaped building used by the military for storage, supplies, and barracks
Rations –	a fixed amount of food, gasoline, and other goods allowed
Rear –	in this case, the part of the military furthest away from the battle action
Reconnaissance –	to survey a region to locate troops, an enemy, or to gain strategic information about an area
Recruit –	a newly enlisted soldier
Retraining –	to teach previously learned behaviors and skills
Regulation –	the required or correct type
Reinforcements –	additional soldiers and weapons to strengthen position
Reveille –	military wake-up signal such as sounding a brass bugle
Scout work –	scout dogs and handlers sent out

	ahead to gather military intelligence
Sentry work –	sentry dogs and handlers stand guard to protect an area
Sicily –	island in the Mediterranean Sea off the southern coast of Italy
Sickbay –	infirmary aboard a ship for those who are sick
Sights –	the part of a gun that helps to aim
Silver Star –	award for acts of gallantry and bravery in action against the enemy
Sortie –	operational military flight
Starboard bow –	the right-hand front end of a ship and the *port bow* is the left-hand front side
Stern –	the rear part of a ship and the farthest distance from the bow
Submarine –	an armed warship capable of operating under water
Taps –	song played by bugler usually at sunset when the flag was lowered
Third Infantry – Division	a division is comprised of approximately 8 to 12 battalions; are basically self-sustaining; and usually led by Major Generals
Torpedoes –	cigar-shaped, underwater explosive missiles
Tracer –	bullet, cannon, or missile that is visible during flight because of flames or sparks it emits
Tracking –	when a dog follows a scent on

the ground

Troop transport – ship — large vessel carrying military personnel

U-boats – German submarine

Vichy – the French state of 1941-1944 that collaborated with Nazi Germany. *Free French* forces were based in London at the beginning of the war and opposed the Vichy government

Victory garden – people grew their own fruits and vegetables so that more farm-grown food would be available for the troops fighting the war

War bonds – certificate issued by the United States government promising to repay the money at a later date at a fixed rate of interest. Over 85 million Americans bought war bonds to help fund the war.

War dog – dog recruited and trained to serve in the armed forces

War dog platoon – a platoon comprised of war dogs and their handlers

War Dog – Training Center — place where war dogs were trained. The first one was in Front Royal, Virginia

War games – simulated war played with mock battles and skirmishes

Whelping box – secure place for a mother dog to tend to her puppies

Wildcats – the F-4 Wildcat was the standard fighter plane at the beginning of

	World War II. Over 40,000 were produced. It was superseded by the F-6 Hellcat
Winston Churchill –	beloved Prime Minister of Great Britain during that country's darkest hours of World War II
Wolf pack –	a group of submarines acting as a unit
Working collar –	a leather buckle collar worn by war dogs while working
Yanks –	slang for Yankee—refers to US citizen

ABOUT THE REAL CHIPS

Chips was born and raised in Pleasantville, New York, in Westchester County. In 1942, at the age of two, he was enlisted in the United States Army through *Dogs for Defense*. He received his boot camp training at the War Dog Training School in Front Royal, Virginia. Chips was eventually paired with handler John P. Rowell. Chips was in the first K-9 detachment to be shipped overseas. Upon arriving in Europe, he and Rowell served with the Third Infantry Division of Patton's Seventh Army. During a beach landing in Sicily, Chips forced the surrender of an enemy pillbox. He was wounded in the attack but continued to fight. Later, during the same invasion, Chips alerted to ten enemy soldiers and participated in their capture. He worked as a sentry dog guarding President Roosevelt and Prime Minister Churchill at the historic Casablanca Conference. While in Italy, Chips was introduced to General Eisenhower, Supreme Commander of the Allied

Forces. When Eisenhower reached toward Chips to give him a pat on the head, the war dog did what he had been trained to do—he nipped the general on the hand!

Chips was the first canine in American history to be awarded the *Distinguished Service Cross* for heroism, the *Purple Heart* for having been wounded in action and the *Silver Star* for bravery. These medals were later revoked by the War Department. Some people believed these high honors should be for humans not animals. However, Chips's commanders eventually awarded him the theater ribbon with an arrowhead for his assault landing at Sicily and a battle star for each of the eight campaigns in which he served.

Although many of the details in this book are *fictionalized*, many of Chips's adventures are based on fact. Chips did pay a surprise visit at Gail's school, bite the local sanitation man, and save young John from drowning. It's also true that after the war many folks thought this gentle giant was a ferocious killer and did not want him living in their little village.

Pal, Mena, and Watch were real dogs in Chips's war dog platoon. Mena had puppies on the troop ship and was returned to the United States. Several of her puppies were kept as mascots and others were returned to Front Royal to be trained as *war dogs*. Sadly, Pal was killed in action on April 23, 1945 while protecting the men in his platoon.

Chips was released from active duty in 1945 and returned to his owners, Mr. and Mrs. Edward Wren in Pleasantville. Photographers and journalists accompanied him on his long train ride home. He adapted to